PENGUIN METRO READS
THE BEST COUPLE EVER

Novoneel Chakraborty is the bestselling author of ten romantic thriller novels and one short story collection, *Cheaters*. The Forever series was listed among *Times of India*'s most stunning books of 2017; it was also featured among Amazon's memorable books the same year. The two books remained on the bestseller list for ten weeks straight and *Forever Is a Lie* was one of the highest selling books of 2017 on Flipkart. While the third instalment in the Stranger trilogy, *Forget Me Not, Stranger*, debuted as the No. 1 bestseller across India, the second, *All Yours, Stranger*, ranked among the top five thrillers on Amazon India. *Black Suits You* also remained among the top five thrillers on Amazon for fifteen weeks. The Stranger trilogy has been translated into six languages. It will soon be adapted into a web series. *Cheaters* will be available in Hindi as well.

Known for his twists, dark plots and strong female protagonists, Novoneel Chakraborty is also called the Sidney Sheldon of India by his readers. Apart from novels, Novoneel has written and developed several TV shows such as *Savdhaan India* and *Yeh Hai Aashiqui*. He lives and works in Mumbai.

The Best Couple Ever

NOVONEEL CHAKRABORTY

Penguin
metro reads

An imprint of Penguin Random House

PENGUIN METRO READS

USA | Canada | UK | Ireland | Australia
New Zealand | India | South Africa | China | Singapore

Penguin Metro Reads is part of the Penguin Random House group of companies
whose addresses can be found at global.penguinrandomhouse.com

Published by Penguin Random House India Pvt. Ltd
4th Floor, Capital Tower 1, MG Road,
Gurugram 122 002, Haryana, India

Penguin
Random House
India

First published in Penguin Metro Reads by Penguin Random House India 2018

ISBN 9780143441984

Typeset in Requiem Text by Manipal Digital Systems, Manipal

Printed at Manipal Technologies Limited, India

www.penguin.co.in

MIX
Paper | Supporting
responsible forestry
FSC® C043100

This is a legitimate digitally printed version of the book and therefore might not
have certain extra finishing on the cover.

For the man the world may think is a misfit
but I call him my Hero.

PROLOGUE

October 2018
The Present

She splashed some water on her face, paused, took a breath and then splashed some more. She lifted her head and looked into the small mirror above the basin. She smiled. Her make-up was spoilt. But that wasn't the only thing. She had been stubborn enough to be a *bad girl*.

She still couldn't believe it. She was in Goa with a man she had met three months ago on Instagram. And now they were here, as he'd randomly planned. For her husband, she was at work. But in reality, she had driven to the airport to join the man at the T3 terminal of Indira Gandhi International Airport, New Delhi. The plan was to fly to Goa, spend the entire day together at a small resort on the beach and take the late evening flight back to New Delhi. It had sounded like a forbidden fantasy. And now it was a scandalous reality. What had happened in the resort room for the last three hours was both dark and funny. It was dark because she had tried some raunchy positions that were a first for her, along with the realization that she had a thing for them. It was funny because they were role playing as Batman and Catwoman. Her partner had bought the costumes in Delhi. Till then, she had thought it was a joke. She had burst out laughing on seeing the costumes. Hers even had a tail. But, surprising herself, she enjoyed it.

She removed her make-up and sat on the commode to relieve herself. Then she took a few selfies. The post-coital bliss was evident on her face. Next, she started scrolling through her WhatsApp messages. There was a barrage of texts in her girls' group but none from her husband. She didn't read any of them. She minimized WhatsApp and tapped on the Instagram app instead. There were a few notifications. One of them was a tag. She clicked on it and was shocked out of her wits. Her partner had posted a picture of her in the Catwoman costume—she was on all fours. She didn't know when the photo had been taken. Although she was unrecognizable in the costume, this wasn't a part of the 'deal'. They had never talked about it, but some things are understood, right? It was a clandestine fling! She was getting angrier with every passing second. She hid the picture from her timeline and untagged herself. She stood up and flushed. She wanted an explanation.

But she froze the moment she stepped inside the room. Her partner was lying on the floor in a pool of blood, still wearing the Batman mask. He was naked and his throat was slit. Her blood turned cold; she tried screaming but no sound came out. She wanted to call for help but she didn't. She looked around. There was nobody. In fact, there were no signs of a struggle at all. The main door was also locked from inside. As the reality of the matter sank in, she walked clumsily towards the body. What should she do? She couldn't call the police. She couldn't even call the people who ran the resort. Anything she did would expose her . . . and the fact that she was having an affair. Her whole world would crumble down, just like that. There was nothing that she could do, except . . . pack and run.

With her heart in her mouth, she quickly wore her dress, stuffed everything, including the Catwoman costume, in her bag and dashed out of the room. Thankfully, they had booked their respective tickets and only he had checked into the resort. The plan was to tell the owners that she was his local guest.

She had a lump in her throat. She had covered her face with a scarf and worn big sunglasses when she had arrived. She did the same while leaving. Identifying her wouldn't be that easy, she hoped. Then she wondered as to whom she was kidding. Tracking her down would be easy if someone wanted to. *If someone knew*. Tears pricked her eyes as she walked towards a rent-a-car shop to hire a cab to the airport.

A few minutes after she left, the man in the room sat up and wiped off the fake blood from his throat. He removed his mask and picked up a packet of cigarettes and a lighter from a nearby table. *All's well that ends well*, he thought as he blew rings of smoke in rapid succession.

* * *

Couple Talks

Ashvamedha Chauhaan flicked the lighter a few times before a spark appeared. Then he held the piece of paper that he was holding in his left hand above the flame. As it caught fire, a smile appeared on his face like that of a warrior who had finally accepted that his arsenal was too small, his hopes too insignificant and his expectations too delusional for the war he had thought he would fight. And win. In no time, the piece of paper turned into ash. It was his PGDBM certificate from a reputed business school. The remains joined the heap of ashes of the rest of his certificates. He picked up a fistful and smeared it on his face. He looked at his reflection in the small mirror above his study table and laughed a little madly, as if someone had just told him that he was immortal.

'What are you doing?' It was his wife, Sama Akhtar; she was already in bed.

'Nothing. Just eliminating waste,' he said, rubbing the ash off his face. Then he went inside the bathroom and came out after washing his face, and joined her in bed. He snuggled up to her and put his head on her bosom and closed his eyes. This was his favorite sleeping position, she knew. A moment later, he looked up at her and said, 'I was wondering about the first time we met.'

'Suddenly?' She was surprised.

'Not really. I'll tell you why it struck me. But later. Right now, I want to relive our meet cute even though I've done it a thousand times already.'

'You aren't the only one. I'm also guilty of doing that,' Sama said brightly.

'It was Lucknow,' Ashvamedha closed his eyes, 'I was there with a friend. We were on a bike. We saw this *baarat*; people were dancing like crazy.'

'It was my best friend's brother's marriage.' Sama too closed her eyes.

'Yeah. My friend and I parked the bike and stood by the road to watch the baaratis. That's when I spotted you—the turquoise lehenga, those emerald earrings, the necklace and the maang tika, the matching bangles and the dark mehendi on your hands.'

'All thanks to my best friend. I never really dolled up. But she would and she didn't spare me that night.'

'I couldn't take my eyes off you. You were so beautiful, and as pure as . . . your daily namaaz. I have never told you this before but when I saw you for the first time, I knew you weren't like any other girl. There was this wild wisdom in your eyes. The wild part told me that you had seen too many men to be bluffed easily with those three words—I love you. The wisdom part told me that your experience had led you to conclude that all men were the same. And such conclusions are like icebergs. They are deep-seated. I knew I had to melt them. I had to be that ever-eluding exception in your life. But I also knew I couldn't do it by impressing you with promises, or words, or clichéd romantic actions. And every time I saw you, talked to you, heard you, I understood you weren't the duel you seemed to be. You were a magnanimous war I was up against. A war that could go on for years. Or, who knows, might have gone on for our lives. All I told myself was that I'm not giving up.'

'One of those things you say . . .' Sama blushed.

'I mean what I say.' They looked at each other and then Ashvamedha continued, 'And when I saw you approaching me I was frozen. You handed me your sandals assuming I was one of the baaratis.'

'And you even took them!'

'I took them because when you left and joined the baarat, I was still frozen but my heart had melted. My friend and I followed you till the baarat entered the wedding venue and you came back to take the sandals. You thanked me.'

'Honestly, I didn't even register your face then,' she said.

He looked at her. Her eyes were open. They burst out laughing.

'You were supposed to tell me why you suddenly thought about that night.'

Ashvamedha grew quiet for a few seconds before saying, 'I met a few old friends of mine.' He was pensive before correcting himself, 'Didn't meet but connected. Yes, connected is the right word.'

'How?'

'Recently while talking to one of my students in school I realized it was high time I took social media seriously. So, I made an account on Facebook and looked up some old buddies. I connected with all of them.'

'That's great. How are they?'

'They are all fine, rather happy. You know, they were playing a contest called the 'best couple ever' when I got in touch with them.'

'What's that?'

'If two people think they are the best couple ever, then all they have to do is post a picture of themselves for the next week or so. The picture with the maximum number of likes will be declared the best.'

'Isn't that silly? What can a photograph prove about a relationship?'

'Their enthusiasm tells me it is anything but silly. I looked up a few other social media platforms too. There is an app that lets you upload your pictures, you know. Then people like your pictures or follow your profile. You can interact with them and become friends. It's all an attempt to connect with everyone who is no one.'

'These are photographers posting their work?' Sama was curious.

'Not necessarily. For example, one of my friends has lakhs of followers and she calls herself an influencer.'

'Whom does she influence?'

'I'm not sure. I saw her pictures—they are mostly of her day-to-day life—and some videos where she is either dancing to a song or mouthing some movie dialogues. She is a cyber-celeb of sorts.'

'Is it that easy to become a celeb these days?'

'Seems like it. People are okay peddling a false image of themselves to ones that are okay accepting that image as the truth. That's why they are influencers, I guess, because people are that gullible nowadays.' Ashvamedha paused and added, 'But everything has a short-term effect and a long-term effect. The short-term effect is connecting with loads of new people and the long-term effect, I'm afraid, is a disconnection with one's self and the immediate surrounding. For example, if I'd allowed myself to be sucked into that fake cyber world with its pseudo aspirations, then I wouldn't have been here with my head on your bosom and reliving the night we had first met.'

They fell silent as Sama ran her fingers through his hair.

'Can you tell me, Sama, what's man's greatest invention after the wheel?'

'Electricity?'

'No.'

'Telephone?'

'No.'

'Then?'

'Social media. The wheel took man from one place to another. Social media takes a person from one identity to another.' He laughed. Sama shrugged. He stopped, saying, 'Nothing. I was just wondering who would win the best couple ever contest among my friends. Sorry, I mean my *happy* friends.' Ashvamedha closed his eyes. A diabolical smile spread on his face as he thought about all that could happen if he implemented what seemed like a foolproof plan.

'What do you think? Who will win?' He heard Sama ask.

'I don't know. They all seem so happy. So damn happy! As if they are all living the perfect life. All of them.'

'Good for them,' Sama said.

'Hmm,' Ashvamedh mumbled, and holding Sama tighter, wondered *how could someone be so happy all the time? I'm sure the cyber world is only an edited version of one's life that people put up for everyone's consumption.* He sighed. *Well, I'll soon find out.* These were his last thoughts before he drifted off to sleep.

BOOK 1

The Couples

1

Kashvi Khandelwal Basu and Dr Parth Basu
(March 2018 to October 2018)
Nagai (Fine Dining and Bar)
Sector-29
Gurugram
9.45 p.m.

'I can't believe she has thrown a party for having 3 lakh followers on Instagram. I mean, seriously! How silly is that?' Kashvi whispered, sipping her mojito. The spite in her voice was nothing new. Not for Dhrithi at least who had excused herself and gone to the restroom. And Sanisha, whose ears Kashvi was speaking into, knew that the latter was just jealous. She would do the same if she had amassed 3 lakh followers. Right now, she was stuck on 1,08,000. After all, both Kashvi and Dhrithi were social media celebrities and influencers. Sanisha was neither, nor was she interested. Unfortunately, she had to be an unwilling confidant for both Dhrithi and Kashvi, especially when they were bitching about each other.

'See, what she added to her story from the washroom?' Kashvi turned her iPhone X's screen towards Sanisha. It had Dhrithi's mirror selfie with the text: *missing my baby, see you in an hour*, along with three kiss emojis. Sanisha didn't know how to react. From what she knew of Kashvi, she would've done the same the moment she reached home or got into her car. Kashvi didn't wait for Sanisha to react. She withdrew herself a bit as she saw Dhrithi coming.

'What's up, ladies?' Dhrithi said, settling down.

'Nothing. I was just telling Sanisha my likes have crossed 50k in my last "best couple ever" pic on Instagram. My fastest 50k till now. Just eight hours!' Kashvi said enthusiastically.

Every group of friends has that person who is always trying to fit in. In the present trio, Sanisha was the one. It was interesting how they had come to know each other. While Sanisha and her live-in partner, and Dhrithi and her husband had done their MBA together, Kashvi had come to know the two ladies once she had married Parth—the other MBA batchmate of the lot. Since the husbands were pals and always hanging out with each other, be it in office or on trips abroad, it was an unsaid rule that the wives should get along as well. And so Sanisha found herself sitting with Kashvi and Dhrithi, trying not to take sides and yet pretending that she was interested in both.

'Young men these days!' Dhrithi said, finishing her cosmopolitan.

'What happened?' Kashvi asked.

'Remember that bikini pic of mine from the Maldives last year?' Dhrithi scrolled down to that picture and showed it to

Kashvi and Sanisha. Dhrithi was in an orange bikini, which she had bought from Miami a year ago. Her skin was shimmering in the sun as she sat with her toned legs half immersed in a swimming pool overlooking a clear sky. Kashvi remembered the picture very well—it was what had motivated her to join a gym the very next day.

'This picture,' Dhrithi said, 'had 5k comments. And most were from young men who wanted to date me. Just imagine!' The surprise was feigned. What Dhrithi was really telling them was—I'm still a wet dream for a lot of young men. Sanisha couldn't care less. Suddenly, Kashvi exclaimed loudly, 'Oh, wow! A certified follower!' Sanisha was sure that the notification must have come earlier that day but the announcement was made in such a way that it seemed as if it had happened seconds ago.

'My thirty-third certified follower on Insta. How many do you have, Dhrithi?' Kashvi was pretty sure she had more certified followers than her.

'The last time I checked it was forty,' Dhrithi said matter-of-factly. Kashvi tried to be nonchalant; Sanisha suppressed her laughter.

'BTW, who is this new certified follower?' Dhrithi asked.

'Varun Tomar!' Kashvi declared with a hint of pride.

'That famous stand-up comedian?' Dhrithi asked.

'Yeah. I've subscribed to him on YouTube as well,' Kashvi said.

'Oh! He is already following me,' Dhrithi said in an I-am-not-interested-any-more way.

Sanisha was dying to leave. She turned to ask Kashvi if they were done but Kashvi had other plans. 'Hi, friends, thought of doing a sudden Insta live. Well, I'm right now at Nagai with my two soul sisters. Say hi to Dhrithi and Sanisha.' She turned the phone towards them. Dhrithi waved, beaming, while Sanisha smiled tightly. 'We are enjoying our ladies' night out with some awesome drinks. What are you guys doing?' Kashvi then turned the phone around to let her followers see the drinks that they had ordered and then apologized since most of it was over. As she went on, Sanisha told Dhrithi that they should ask for the bill. She knew this sudden live video was done to get an edge over Dhrithi's bikini pic. Kashvi was a born attention-seeker. And she was always jealous of other people. Sanisha couldn't wait to get home and tell her partner about the ludicrous night and laugh about it together.

As one of the waiters brought the bill, Kashvi was still live on Instagram. Unknown to her, a certain couple was also watching it from their bedroom. Minutes later, both Dhrithi and Kashvi got a new follower each. They didn't bother to see who it was.

2

Kashvi's husband, Parth, was running on the treadmill when she reached home. They lived in a sprawling 4 BHK penthouse, which Parth had gifted her on their third marriage anniversary. Every nook and corner of the penthouse spoke of élan, eclectic international furnishing and fine wooden furniture. The colour theme for the entire penthouse was a mix of turquoise and white, Kashvi's favourites. All she could think about when she saw the fully furnished penthouse for the first time were the words her family astrologer had said while looking at her forehead in Kolkata. *She will live like a queen.* And she was.

At thirty-four, Dr Parth Basu was a successful third generation oral and maxillofacial surgeon. His grandfather had been close friends with several former prime ministers. His father had carried on the legacy not only by continuing to be in the same profession but also by contesting elections. It took the Basu family directly to the power centre of Delhi—Lutyens'. Parth, an only son, was sent to Russia for his undergrad medical studies and later to the UK for his masters and a surgical diploma. It was but obvious for him to join his father at Basu Memorial

Multi-Specialty Hospital in Chanakyapuri, New Delhi. He also did an MBA, knowing well that his hospital wouldn't just require his medical skills but also a fair knowledge of business.

Kashvi came from a middle-class Marwari family; her grandparents had settled in Kolkata forty years ago. From owning a small clothes shop in Burrabazar, her family went on to open a fancy store in New Market. Throughout her childhood, her parents favoured her brother more than her and her sister, who grew up being deliberately neglected. The first time a birthday was celebrated at home was when her brother turned a year old. The first time her family planned a trip together was when her brother was able to walk. Her father bought a cycle, the first, for her brother when he could ride it. A tutor was hired when her brother needed one. The first time pocket money was distributed among the siblings was when her brother asked for it. While her sister eventually got used to the discrimination, Kashvi couldn't. She was acutely aware of strangulating her wishes during her childhood years. Everything was always divided among the three, the lion's share going to her brother, which frustrated her no end.

Kashvi grew up to be a beautiful girl. She realized this when she joined college and unintentionally became the most sought-after girl . . . till Siddharth, her senior, asked her out. She wanted to think about it but was forced to say yes by her friends, which surprisingly turned out to be the best decision of her life. Not because she loved Siddharth, but because that is when she understood what a beautiful girl like her truly deserved—full-time pampering. In no time, she became a high-maintenance girlfriend, who needed care and attention from her partner mostly in the form of material things. Siddharth did whatever he could, and when he couldn't, she dumped him. Then it was Raghav, Mohit, Rohan, Anirban and Sandip. She dated at least two boys in a year. Soon, she had to get a separate wardrobe for the gifts she squeezed out of those dalliances. For others, she was a heartless girl who only toyed with boys' hearts, but for her own self, Kashvi—as she finally understood what the childhood frustration had turned her into—was a compulsive and unapologetic gold-digger.

'Hi, baby!' She greeted Parth as he stepped down from the treadmill all sweaty.

'How was the night out, babe?' Parth asked, wiping his face with a towel.

Kashvi walked up to him and picked up his phone, tapping on a health app. Last month, Parth's blood pressure had shot up due to work-related stress. Since then, Kashvi had been monitoring his health through this app. She'd read somewhere that high blood pressure could lead to erectile dysfunction if unchecked. The last thing she wanted was to be a queen with a king who couldn't get it up.

'Happy?' Parth asked as Kashvi put his phone down.

'A wife who has an obedient hubby? More than happy, sweetheart.' She smiled at him and said, 'Go get a shower. I'll see to it that your dinner is ready by then.'

'I've an observation though.' Parth slowly walked towards her. She knew something naughty was coming up.

9

'If something as hot as this,' he grabbed her butt over her red one-piece dress and continued, 'is already here, why wait for dinner?'

Kashvi gave him an acknowledging smile and said, 'Are you objectifying your wife, mister?'

'Why? Don't I have the right to?' Parth embraced her, which made her feel funny between her legs.

'Maybe you do. But do you know what I'm wearing underneath today?' she asked him, and could feel his penis poking her.

'That red lingerie we bought from Amsterdam?'

'No, I'm wearing a sanitary pad.'

It took Parth a few seconds to realize what she had said and what it meant.

'Come on!' he was disappointed.

'I wish, but I don't control my chumming, babe. So, head for the shower. You'll have to make do with only steaming vegetables tonight.'

Parth made a face and left for the washroom. Kashvi called the help and asked him to prepare dinner. By the time she had changed, dinner was ready. She took pictures of the different dishes on the table and posted one on Instagram with a text: *even after a ladies' night out, a wife is a wife is a wife*. The fact that she had neither cooked the food nor served it was, like always, edited out. She posted it with fifteen hashtags, after which likes and comments kept pouring in, declaring Kashvi to be the best wife ever.

After dinner, Parth chose to read a business journal on his Kindle, while Kashvi logged into Instagram to check her notifications. There were 1042 likes and as many comments since the last time she had checked—thirty-two minutes ago to be precise. But all the likes and comments were from one person only. She tapped on that man's profile. He had 309 posts, 710 followers and was following 310 handles. His name was Nihit Tandon. She tapped on his latest picture. *Handsome*, was the first adjective that came to her mind. The next second, she received a message from Nihit.

3

Dear Kashvi ma'am,

This is Nihit. I'm a part of a YouTube group called 'The Sensations'. You can check us out on http://www.youtube.com/TheSensations. Basically, we interview up-and-coming social media celebrities. Since you are clearly ruling the hearts of so many people on Instagram, we were hoping to interview you at your convenience. It will be a video interview at Culina 44 in Taj City Centre in Gurugram. All expenses borne by us. Waiting anxiously for your positive response.

Thanks and regards,
Nihit Tandon

Kashvi read the message for the umpteenth time. Usually she didn't respond to Instagram messages because of two reasons: one, there were too many of them. And second, she believed that celebs didn't respond to fans' messages even when they were free. She got back to only certain business requests from brands or companies that were interested in collaborating with her for their products. To date Kashvi had collaborated with only a cosmetic company, a phone cover store and a junk jewellery store—local brands trying to find a footing in social media. She'd never been interviewed before. The request made her feel important, which was what she'd been seeking from life all this time. This was also why she hadn't stuck around with one man for too long. She believed the kind of importance a man gave a woman in the form of romance died with time. It was better to hop from one relationship to another than grow roots into any one of them. Of course, this involved heartbreaks, mostly for the men, but then if one didn't cry in love, one didn't deserve to love either, or so Kashvi thought.

But Kashvi had a totally different definition for marriage. For her, marriage was for keeps. It wasn't something to walk out of. Thus, before getting in, one had to weigh everything. Especially what one really wanted from one's marriage. No cheating in that. For whatever the world might say, marriage has always been the most understated business model. If it was only and solely about companionship, then one didn't need the concept of marriage. But since childhood, Kashvi knew that marriage was about a lot of things. Things that were important; things that validated one's self.

Kashvi always knew what she wanted from her husband. He had to be 'well-settled'. It was better to cry in an Audi than in an autorickshaw. She didn't want to work after getting married; she also didn't want any restrictions on her freedom—freedom to wear what she wanted, eat what she wanted and do what she wanted.

She was working at a call centre in Hyderabad after her graduation so she could sponsor her own little 'high-life' perks, when she took the life-changing decision of accompanying her roommate to her cousin's marriage in Delhi. That's where she met Parth.

She read Nihit's message a few times and checked the mentioned YouTube channel. It was there all right. The Sensations were indeed a YouTube channel featuring different social media celebs, be it NRI singers, stand-up comedians, Musical.ly stars or others like them. She could almost see her interview while checking the other videos. And the expression on Dhrithi's face when the latter would be told about the interview. It was only the next morning, after Parth had had his breakfast and left for the hospital, that she decided to reply while getting a pedicure and hair spa done in an expensive salon.

Hi, Nihit,

Thanks for considering me.

She erased the word 'considering'. Sounded like she had low self-esteem.

Hi, Nihit,

Thanks for inviting me.

She erased it again. Inviting sounded like nobody ever did.

Hi, Nihit,

Sure. How do we take this forward?

She smiled. Simple, straight and totally 'celeb-type'. She sent the message and then took a mirror selfie. She posted it on Instagram with a note: *be yourself? But what to do when the post-salon look is sexier?* Within half a minute, likes and comments started pouring in:

—*Aww, you look naturally beautiful!*

—*You are my inspiration!*

—*Such natural beauty!*

These comments were her emotional sedatives. A response from Nihit came some time later while her body spa was on.

Dear Kashvi ma'am,

We are delighted that you're interested. As stated earlier, the interview will happen at Culina 44. Please confirm the day and time. We shall happily make ourselves available.

Thanks and regards,

Nihit

She read it while going to an art exhibition at Triveni Kala Sangam, Mandi House. She didn't have much taste in art, but she wanted people to think that she did. Her perception of her own self was heavily dependent on other people's perception of her. She bought a few paintings—the more obscure the better—from the exhibition. It was only while she was having coffee at Starbucks in Select Citywalk Mall, Saket, with Parth, who had taken a break from his hospital duties, that she responded to Nihit.

I'm free tomorrow between 3 to 6 p.m.

She wondered if three hours would be good enough for a video interview.

'We could have met near my hospital as well,' Parth said.

'I've been wanting to check in to Select City for a while now,' Kashvi said, readying the portrait mode of her phone camera. She clicked a picture of the two cups of coffee, which had two words on them: 'best' and 'couple'.

Sudden coffee cravings. Who else to share with if not bae-hubby! She followed the text with six hearts and then uploaded the photo on Instagram, tagging Parth. While scrolling down her feed, she saw that a couple of hours ago Dhrithi had uploaded a picture, with twenty-five hashtags, of her in some snowy place in New Zealand; she was skiing in hot pants. *Who skies in hot pants?* Kashvi wondered and immediately edited her latest post and added ten more hashtags. She then went back to Dhrithi's New Zealand photo. A smile appeared on her face when she found that she was leading in both likes and comments.

'Sometimes I feel instead of me you should have taken those *saath pheras* with the phone,' Parth quipped while sipping his coffee. He knew his wife's obsession with social media was nothing new.

'I can also say the same. You should have taken the pheras with the blueprint of your hospital. Do you even remember the last time we met for coffee during a week day?'

Parth knew better than to argue. He was about to say something when Kashvi's phone buzzed with an incoming message. She checked it.

Thank you so much, Kashvi ma'am. Looking forward to meeting you in person. It was from Nihit.

'What happened?' Parth asked as she was smiling at her phone.

'I've an interview tomorrow. Don't you know, Dr Basu, your wife is a celebrity?'

'As long as people don't end up thinking she has a doctor for a manager,' he said.

'Tch, tch, tch. Poor baby. I'll never do that to you.' She pulled one of his cheeks. He smiled sheepishly.

Kashvi didn't know that Nihit had texted her from the trial room of a store above Starbucks. He seemed happy looking at himself in the outfit he was going to wear the next day. Then he texted her again.

Sorry to bother you, ma'am, but may I have your number, please? Will help us in coordination. Thanks.

Two minutes later Kashvi texted her number. Nihit tried saving the number but his contact list already had it. Still, he had to ask. *When it comes to women, politeness is the key,* he murmured to himself.

17

4

Kashvi had thought that she would be intentionally late but then decided not to after getting a call from Nihit.

'Hello, ma'am, Nihit here.'

'Hi, Nihit,' she said, wondering if she was sounding casual enough for a celeb.

'Ma'am, we have reached the place. Waiting for you now. Hope to see you on time.'

Nihit's servile tone impressed her enough to confirm that she would be on time. She took a small video of herself sitting in her Audi and put it on her Instagram story with the text: *heading towards my first interview! Keep waiting for something exciting*. A minute later, Dhrithi called her up inquiring what the interview was about and for whom, which put Kashvi in the right mood.

In her blue Bebe dress, Gucci heels, a Michael Kors handbag and her recently permed hair, Kashvi looked quite a stunner. At Culina 44, she was walking towards the reception, when she was intercepted by Nihit.

'Hello, Kashvi ma'am!' Kashvi immediately recognized Nihit from his profile picture on Instagram but didn't want to make it obvious.

'Nihit?' She feigned a vague recognition.

'Of course!' He had a winning smile. And, as Kashvi noticed, he was little more handsome and younger than his Instagram profile picture. Nihit was around six feet tall and was wearing a white shirt with a turquoise jacket and denims. He didn't look like a gym-rat but Kashvi could guess he had a good physique underneath the clothes. Especially the way in which his jacket fitted the shoulders and the shirt stuck to his well-toned abs.

'That's my favourite colour,' she said, eyeing his jacket.

'Thank you, ma'am. This is for you.' He gave her a bouquet of a rare variety of flowers.

'Oh my God! Are they Parrot's Beak?' Kashvi couldn't hide her astonishment.

'They are. You had posted these in one of your Instagram posts. I thought you would like them.'

'I absolutely love them! Thank you, Nihit,' she said, not able to take her eyes off the flowers. She'd been trying to get some for herself but this was a helluva surprise, she thought.

'If you don't mind, ma'am, can we please sit there till my team is here,' Nihit asked, gesturing towards a reserved table.

'Sure,' Kashvi said and followed Nihit to the table. He pulled a chair for her, she thanked him and sat down.

'Where's your team?' she asked.

'They are on their way. Actually, they are coming from Noida. And there's some traffic so . . . let me check,' Nihit said and made a phone call.

'Fifteen minutes more,' he told Kashvi, disconnecting the call.

'Sure,' she smiled. A waiter came to ask if they would prefer mineral water. Nihit nodded and asked Kashvi, 'Would you like to drink something?'

'Maybe a virgin mojito,' Kashvi said. The waiter nodded and left.

Kashvi started surfing her social media accounts on the phone when Nihit said, 'I'm really feeling lucky to be with you. Like I've been following you for some time now on Instagram. And you truly are an influencer as your "about me" section says.'

Kashvi looked up, flashed another beatific smile and said, 'Never knew I could influence a man as well.'

'But you did! You helped me understand that the perfect wife concept isn't a myth. It's true. I really hope to get married to you,' he looked earnestly at her.

'Huh?'

'I'm sorry. I meant to someone like you. Talking to you like this is making me nervous actually.'

This was the first time Kashvi had met someone who was so much in awe of her. She was savouring the feeling. It switched on the rarely used modest button in her.

'Oh, that's okay. Don't be nervous. I'm sure if you look properly, you'll find someone like me.'

'I don't think so. I'm confident you are the only one.'

She smiled. He had said what she had wanted him to say. Almost 3–4 minutes went by without the two of them saying anything. Kashvi was busy scrolling through timelines on her phone. Suddenly, she lifted her head to find Nihit staring at her. She felt a tad uncomfortable, but she didn't show it. The awkwardness was broken by the waiter who brought her the mojito.

'May I ask you something, ma'am?' Nihit asked. Kashvi nodded, stirring the mojito.

'What does happiness mean for you?'

Kashvi was taken aback by the question.

'Don't worry, ma'am. I'm not the interviewer. It's just that I had wanted to ask you this for some time now.'

Kashvi quickly thought about something intellectual. 'For me, happiness is being in charge of your life. As long as I'm in charge, I'm happy.'

'Brilliant!' Nihit said.

'Could you check how far your team is now?' she asked, sipping the mojito.

'Sure, ma'am,' Nihit said and immediately made another call. He talked for a few seconds and then told Kashvi that the team was almost here. She gave him an acknowledging smile, excused herself to the washroom and came back after a little touch-up. The moment she sat down, Nihit apologized.

'I'm sorry,' he said.

'For?'

'I lied to you.'

'As in?' Kashvi frowned.

'I'm not part of any YouTube channel. I'm a commercial pilot with Jet-Set Airlines. But I'm a true fan of yours. I only wanted to meet you. See you in person. Sit in front of you. But I knew you wouldn't have agreed to meet me just like that. Hence, the lie. Please forgive me. I'm only a harmless fan who had desired to meet you. That's all.'

Kashvi didn't say anything. She was shocked. How easily she'd fallen for the whole story and made a fool of herself. Nihit suddenly went down on his knees. Kashvi looked around to find everyone staring at them. Although she liked such dramatic gestures this time she felt acutely embarrassed. She assumed the gesture was a result of Nihit's guilt. But for Nihit, it was part of his research.

Before she could say anything, she heard voices. Turning around, she saw five people with two cameras and a boom mic approaching them. There was a woman in that group who was the best-dressed.

'They're here,' Nihit said, getting up.

'Who?' For a moment, Kashvi was clueless.

'The Sensations team. They'll take your interview.'

'But you said you lied to me. What's going on?'

'I only lied about my involvement with The Sensations. The rest of it is true. I did want to meet you but I also made sure the interview happened. I think someone like you deserves it.'

As the crew started setting up their equipment for the interview, Kashvi's irk-turned-anger faded into I-don't-know-what-to-tell-this-man-now.

'I'm a fan of yours, ma'am. How can I do anything to displease you?' Nihit said.

Kashvi couldn't read much into his expression.

'Hi, ma'am, I'm Ronita and I'll be taking your interview,' the well-dressed woman came up to her and said. As the interview began, Nihit left her side and went to stand at some distance. In twenty minutes, the interview was over; all done in one take. When Kashvi stood up, looking for Nihit, he was nowhere to be seen.

* * *

Couple Talks

'So, according to Kashvi, happiness is when things happen of your own free will,' Ashvamedha said. He was shaving, peering into his reflection in a small mirror on the wall.

'That's such a limiting definition of happiness, no?' Sama asked. He looked at her through the mirror. She was sitting in bed, reading a book.

'Definitions are always limiting. But I know what you mean: what about those times when one is just lucky? When fortunate things happen to someone even when they have no control over the situations whatsoever?'

'Precisely,' Sama added.

'Anyway, I'll take care of that. But what I couldn't understand were the people who worship her as their role model, inspiration, aspiration, etc., based on her photographs only. I mean what is this world that we are living in—where heroes don't even have to do anything to become a hero except for putting up heavily edited photographs online?' Ashvamedha paused and then said, 'Isn't that disturbing?'

'Very disturbing. If we have pseudo heroes, we will have pseudo virtues and accordingly, a fake society,' Sama said.

'What I don't understand is what makes people fall for all this? Why can't they see through such facades? How can people be so dumb and gullible? Contrary to belief, are human beings then not the most intelligent of all animals but the stupidest?' Ashvamedha continued after a thoughtful pause.

'Yes, the Internet revolution is the next big turning point in the history of mankind. Unfortunately, it has stripped us of a lot of things that we were once sure of about ourselves. Or thought we were sure of.'

'My father's hero was this man named Jamil *Chacha* who, as legend had it, once took fifteen bullets from the British. A group of *goras* had planned to gang-rape women in the locality that Jamil Chacha stayed in, accusing them of taking part in anti-establishment uprisings. The women were able to escape because chacha distracted the goras. For my father, to stand up for someone's honour was an act of heroism.

'My own hero has been Kapil Dev, the cricketer, because he, along with his team, made us—Indians—believe that we could win as a sporting nation at the highest level,' he paused, a mocking smile playing on his lips. 'And then there are today's teenagers whom I teach. I once asked a student of mine who her hero was. She mentioned a man whom I'd never heard of, though the buzz in the class after she took his name was telling enough. I asked her what he had done to inspire her. You know what she told me?'

'What?'

'That this so-called hero of hers "looks insanely cute, has a killer body and uploads videos of himself through some app where he mouths either someone else's songs or dialogues in a funny manner". Oh, and "he has won three reality shows". When I read about this person later on Google, I realized one of those reality shows was only about bitching and pretending to be a simpleton. That's her hero. Believe me, Sama, I felt nauseated.'

'Of course, we can't say that all teens are like that,' Sama said.

'Thankfully we can't. We shouldn't. And I hope we are right in assuming there is a clear majority of teenagers who do not have such a screwed-up, mediocre and frivolous idea of who a hero is.'

'Times are changing, Ashva. Times are changing. We are making a joke out of the most powerful tool we ever invented. So I feel,' Sama said.

'I know. And I agree.' Done with his shaving, Ashvamedha splashed some water on his face. He put his razor inside the shaving kit, wiped his face with a towel and, taking the aftershave lotion with him, approached Sama. She held out her palm. He squeezed out some of the lotion on it and leaned towards her. She applied it on his face and inhaled the scent deeply.

'I love this fragrance!' she said.

'It's not the aftershave. It's your touch,' Ashvamedha said, kissing her hand.

'One of those things you say,' she blushed.

'I mean what I say,' he said and went back to keep the lotion inside the shaving kit. Remembering something, he turned around with an amused smile on his face, 'You remember I told you how good I was at chess during school?'

25

'I remember but you never played it afterwards.'

'That's right. During the time I did I was famous for one thing—I always trumped my opponent in thirteen moves.' The smile on Ashvamedha's face was infectious enough to appear on Sama's as well.

'And you are already done with three moves in Kashvi's case,' she said.

Ashvamedha's smile widened. A warm, winning smile it was.

5

The interview had fetched over 175k views in a week—the highest among all the other videos that The Sensations had uploaded on their channel. It also earned Kashvi an additional 50k followers within a span of four days on Instagram. She didn't tell anyone about the incident with Nihit. She thought it was best left out of the narrative. It was better for people, especially Dhrithi, to assume that The Sensations had approached her on their own.

'Obviously because of my Insta-popularity,' she claimed in front of Parth while they were on their way for a couple spa massage. The topic had come up after Parth found many of his relatives commenting on a video featuring Kashvi. Although she had told him about it, he had, as was typical of him, forgotten about it. Not that it mattered to Kashvi. The thing that she liked the best about Parth was that he wasn't an intrusive husband. He was either busy at the hospital or playing golf with his friends on his day off or catching up on the latest in world politics, club soccer and Indian economy over some fine wine. He never checked her phone or asked her whereabouts. At best, he was a caring husband but never a possessive one.

There was a casual detachment in everything Parth did. He would surprise her on her birthday or their anniversary by booking a high-end dinner or flying her off to some exotic location abroad. But his one special brownie point as a husband was that he was submissive to her. Whenever there was a fight, it was always Parth who apologized and made peace irrespective of whose fault it was. Kashvi's word was always the last.

Parth was an ideal husband for Kashvi. The only con in the relationship was that he wasn't very sexual. They had a normal sex life, but she couldn't remember the last time she didn't have to touch herself to climax after having a session with him. Not that it bothered Kashvi, except when the moment occurred. She had never told Parth about it. If he could give her so much, she often introspected, then she could at least take care of his male ego with ease. So, in bed it was always 'fuck me tiger, fuck me bad' till Parth came and Kashvi excused herself to the washroom to masturbate. Given a choice, Kashvi would marry Parth again. She could stay alive with less sex but not less luxury.

The following Saturday she went to Club South Patio for a swim after Dhrithi told her they hadn't swam for a while. They asked Sanisha to join them but the latter cited some work-related reason and opted out.

'I don't know what's wrong with Sanisha,' Kashvi said. She was in the changing room with Dhrithi.

'Why, what happened?' Dhrithi asked.

'She doesn't go to the spa, for a swim, or for a movie and rarely joins us on night-outs. She isn't even active on social media. But look at Adhik. He is so ... so ...' Kashvi was trying to fish for the right word.

'Opposite?' Dhrithi tried to help.

'Yeah. Opposite!'

'Do you think they will ever get married? Or do you think eventually this "opposite" thing will eat their relationship up?' Dhrithi asked, ready in her lime-coloured bikini.

'I've my doubts. I think they'll separate. I don't think Indian men are still psychologically trained to understand what a live-in is from a woman's perspective,' Kashvi said, adjusting her black monokini around her bosom. In the last few months, her breasts had increased from a C cup to D.

'Neither Indian men nor Indian society has any idea. People still believe live-in means a free pass to sex. They don't know that these days a fourteen-year-old girl is better at giving a blow job than most married women. Our men and society will forever be slow at catching up,' Dhrithi said. The two women had come out of their changing rooms and into the lobby. Kashvi discreetly checked out Dhrithi—her bikini first and then her toned café-au-lait legs. She was looking drop-dead sexy. Kashvi was on the verge of asking how she maintained such a killer figure, but decided not to. It would mean openly admitting that she was gorgeous.

'How am I looking?' Dhrithi asked. Kashvi looked at her from head to toe knowing fully well that the question was rhetorical.

'Like always!' she said and walked out with a towel around her waist, hoping the answer was cryptic enough.

Kashvi had already finished half a lap in the pool when she saw Dhrithi clicking a selfie. She knew the picture would not only fetch likes from her current followers but also get her some new ones. There were times when Kashvi craved to post something mildly scandalous but couldn't as her conservative relatives and family members were everywhere. Also, her followers treated her like 'Sita'—the perfect wife. Nobody would like to see her in a bikini unlike Dhrithi who was a 'hot wife' for her followers. She continued swimming as Dhrithi joined her.

After about an hour of swimming, Dhrithi told Kashvi that she was going to change. As she climbed out of the pool, Kashvi saw men's eyes following her till the changing rooms, where she was headed for a shower. *Such a slut*, she murmured, and continued swimming. While climbing out of the pool, she noticed a man in shorts and a tee with a camera covering his face sitting at some distance. She was sure he was trying to take her picture. She quickly climbed up, took her towel, wrapped it around her waist and went straight to the man. He put down his camera. And Kashvi couldn't believe her eyes.

'How dare you click my picture, Nihit?' she demanded, smacking the camera out of his hands. The blow was a little stronger than was intended. The camera flew out from Nihit's hands and on to the ground. The lens cracked. Nihit looked at Kashvi—bewildered.

'Just because you arranged an interview for me claiming to be my fan doesn't mean you can follow me around. What are you doing here? Why are you clicking my pictures? Answer me or I'm calling the police,' Kashvi was genuinely angry.

'What happened, *bhaiya?*' The sweet voice of a girl distracted Kashvi. She turned around to find a girl, probably in her early twenties, in a swimsuit coming towards them. She was beautiful.

'I wasn't clicking you, ma'am. I didn't even notice you till you came up to me. I was clicking my sister. You can check the memory card.'

The girl gasped and her hands flew to her mouth.

'Is that you, Kashvi ma'am?' she looked stunned.

'Even my sister is a big fan of yours, ma'am,' Nihit said, standing up.

'Can I please take a selfie with you, ma'am? Pretty please?' the girl pleaded. Her joy seemed genuine. Kashvi didn't know how to react. She'd made a fool of herself. Compliance was her only redemption. She nodded and posed with the girl and Nihit for a selfie. They thanked her. Nihit went to pick his DSLR up while Kashvi apologized mildly and hurried towards the changing rooms. She didn't want to meet him again.

The next day was Sunday. Parth, Adhik and Satyam had their weekly golf game and then a barbeque brunch at Parth's house. This was a quarterly ritual; the Sunday brunch alternated every month between the three friends. Kashvi had supervised everything to perfection and, satisfied with the barbeque arrangement, was ready to host the three men for brunch. She opened the door when they arrived. There was Parth leading the way, followed by Adhik and Satyam. And then there was a fourth person whom Parth introduced as their new golf buddy: Nihit Tandon. Kashvi told herself she had better be dreaming.

6

'This is Nihit Tandon. He is our new golf buddy,' Parth declared. The other three followed him, greeting Kashvi one at a time.

'Nihit, this is my wife, Kashvi.'

'Hello, ma'am. How are you?'

'Ma'am?' Parth sounded surprised. 'Call her Kashvi. Unless you want to call me sir,' he chuckled at his joke. The other two men smiled obligingly.

'Hello, Kashvi!' Nihit said.

'Hello, Nihit!' Kashvi's throat had gone dry. *What the fuck is this guy up to*, she wondered. However, Nihit looked genuinely surprised.

'Barbeque is ready,' Kashvi said as Nihit closed the door behind him. He had followed the other three men into the living room balcony. It had been redesigned and had a small garden with various ceramic pots and plants. And right in the middle a small barbeque had been set up. The beer bottles were also ready.

'That's like the perfect wife,' Parth said as he noticed the barbeque warming up. There were fish, chicken and mutton.

'Time for food, boys!' Parth yelled. As he, along with Adhik and Satyam, started piling food on the plates, Nihit stood next to them, looking clueless.

'What happened, Nihit?' Parth asked.

'I'm a vegetarian,' he said.

Parth laughed. 'Finally, you get to share your dishes with someone, Kashvi.' Adhik and Satyam beamed. 'Kashvi is the only vegetarian in the entire group,' Parth clarified.

Kashvi had just stepped into the balcony with her bowl of Greek salad. Usually she left the men alone once she was sure of all the preparations. But today was different. She wanted to be present.

'What happened?' she asked.

'Nihit is a veggie,' Adhik said. Nihit smiled matter-of-factly.

'Oh, all right. What do you want to have, Nihit?' she asked.

'It's okay. I'm not that hungry.'

'Juice?' Kashvi asked.

'Yeah, juice is fine.'

Kashvi left and was back in two minutes.

'Here, pomegranate juice for you.'

'Thank you so much.'

As the men started bantering, Kashvi kept glancing at Nihit. But not even once did he look at her, as if it were normal for him to visit her place every third Sunday like Adhik and Satyam.

'Fuck politics for a second. I think I'm going to kidnap this cook of yours. He is so damn good,' Satyam said.

'Kashvi is so glad it's a "he". Else I might have fallen for her.' Parth winked at Satyam while nodding at Kashvi. She gave him a tight smile. And when she glanced at Nihit, she found that his eyes were on her. She knew why.

'Doesn't Kashvi cook?' Nihit asked. Parth stared at him and said in mock seriousness, 'Of course, she does. But nobody can eat her food without becoming my patient.' He laughed loudly, polishing off the chicken and mutton kebabs with frequent sips of Bira.

Kashvi didn't like the jokes. But there was something else she didn't like more.

'I need to use the washroom,' Nihit said.

'Come, I'll show you the way,' Kashvi said, getting up. He followed her to the guest washroom. He was about to enter when the help interrupted him, 'Ma'am, there is no water in this bathroom. I've called the plumber.'

'Oh, that's weird. It was working fine last night. Anyway, you can use the other one,' Kashvi said and directed Nihit to the washroom attached to the master bedroom. No other words were exchanged between them nor did they look at each other.

'The light switch is inside,' she said.

'Thanks,' Nihit said and locked himself inside.

Once he was done, he opened the door and was taken aback to find Kashvi still standing outside.

'Is it really a coincidence that you played golf with my husband today?' she asked.

'Of course! What else could it be?'

'Hmm. Another thing: do I have to tell you not to tell anyone that I don't know how to cook? That the food in the pictures I post on Instagram is made by my cook but I claim to have made them?' she sounded cold.

Nihit watched her closely for a few seconds and said, 'Trust me, Kashvi, I'd never want to harm you in any way.'

'Good. They are waiting for you outside,' she said and walked out of the room.

Nihit quickly looked around. There was a round bed, loads of photos on the wall and a huge LED television on the wall opposite the bed. Next to the bed was a big wooden wardrobe. He made a dash for it. He opened the wardrobe to see Parth's clothes on one side. There wasn't enough time. Nihit took out a bottle of women's perfume from his pocket and kept it between the clothes in such a manner that no one would find it in a hurry. And yet it wouldn't be that difficult to spot it either.

7

'What do you know about Nihit?' Kashvi tried her best to make the question sound as casual as possible. Ensconced at either end of their Lawson sofa, Kashvi, holding a tub of popcorn, and Parth, sipping his favourite beer, were watching a thriller series on Netflix. Parth glanced askance at her on hearing Nihit's name.

'Why do you ask?' he asked, pausing the TV.

It was clear that he didn't know that Nihit was the one who had 'arranged' her interview with The Sensations.

'Just like that. He didn't seem like your type.'

'He beat us all at golf. And he makes good conversation.' Parth sounded slightly in awe of Nihit.

'So, what did he tell you?'

Parth glanced at her again.

'About his wife?' Kashvi asked, knowing fully well that Nihit was a bachelor.

'Oh! Now, I know. You want another member in your kitty team now that we have Nihit.'

Kashvi smiled but inside she was like you-won't-ever-get-it-darling so please answer me.

'He works as a commercial pilot. He is from Gwalior. His parents stay there. He is a bachelor but stays with his sister who works as . . . I don't remember what he said about his sister. But yeah, that's about it.' After a thoughtful pause, he added, 'And, of course, he has been living in Gurugram for some time now.'

Most of the information was the same except for some new ones like his hometown, parents, etc. But Kashvi had a hunch that it wasn't a coincidence that she had bumped into him at the swimming club and later at home.

'Now can we continue watching?' Parth asked. Kashvi nodded. Her mind wasn't on the show any more.

'Wait.' Kashvi came a little closer to him, draped a leg over his and took a photo of their entwined feet and the TV. Then she went back to where she had been sitting and posted the photo on Instagram with a note: *happiness is watching Netflix together*.

A few days later Kashvi went to the swimming club again. She headed to the club office first. Dhrithi had said that she was busy with work so she had decided to go alone.

There were two men lazing around inside the office. They perked up as she approached them.

'How can we help you, madam?' one of them said.

'I want to know about a member,' she said.

'Madam, we aren't allowed to . . .' Before he could finish, a Rs 2000 note was waved in his face.

'Sure, madam,' the man rephrased his sentence, grabbing the note. He turned towards his computer, tapped a few keys and then asked, 'What's the name of the member?'

37

'Nihit Tandon,' she said.

The man quickly typed in the name and pressed enter. There was one Nihit Tandon. He clicked on the profile. All his information—name, age, address, phone number—was there. But all Kashvi was interested in was the date of joining. She carefully read the date. He'd joined some eight months ago.

'Does he come here often?' she asked.

'The security guard will be able to tell you that, madam.'

'All right, but keep your mouth shut about this,' she hissed at them and walked off.

Kashvi wanted to check his sister's membership as well but had no clue what her name was. She left. After an hour of swimming, she decided to go shopping. While her driver was backing the car out of the swimming club, Kashvi thought of asking the guard about Nihit but decided against it at the last moment. *What if the guard tells him that she was enquiring?* She didn't want to come across as someone who was taking an interest in him.

Kashvi told her driver to take her to Ambience Mall in Gurugram and called up Sanisha.

'Hey, what's up? Tell me you are free!' she said.

'Hey, a lot of work pressure, yaar,' Sanisha said.

'Who works so much in an NGO?'

'Really?'

'Okay, I'm sorry. But you are having lunch with me today. Ambience Mall in an hour?'

'Give me an hour and a half before I can join you,' Sanisha said. She didn't want Kashvi's company as much as she wanted a break.

'Done. Love you.' Kashvi disconnected the call. She checked Instagram. She'd put up a picture of herself inside the pool saying: *best way to beat the heat.* It'd already garnered 20k likes and 150 comments. The first comment was Nihit's.

You were looking ravishing. Didn't approach else you might have thought I'm a freak. LOL.

This was the first time he'd commented on a picture of hers. *Did he know she'd gone to the club office as well?* Kashvi glanced at her watch. There was time. On a hunch, she asked the driver to take her to the Golf Club.

It took her half an hour and another Rs 2000 to get his details. He'd joined the club six months ago. But it was only recently that he had met her husband and his friends. He'd joined the swimming club eight months ago but she had stumbled upon him only a few days ago. Was she unnecessarily reading too much into it? Kashvi's phone buzzed with a message.

Leaving now. It was Sanisha.

Cool, see ya! Kashvi hopped into her car and, still trying to make sense of Nihit's story, asked her driver to head to Ambience Mall.

Sanisha knew Kashvi would bore her with shopping. Shopping was something she hated. So, she'd kept her plan simple: she would meet and say she was dying of hunger. After lunch, she would excuse herself citing a work meeting and leave. The plan was executed just like that.

'But I'd to shop, bae,' Kashvi lamented.

'Work, sweetheart. Can't help. Really sorry. I'll make up for this soon,' Sanisha said, hugged Kashvi and took her leave.

Kashvi wandered around the mall, finally deciding to enter the H & M store. She picked up a few tops and palazzos for trial. Near the trial rooms, she was shocked to see Nihit. For a moment, she was sure that he was following her. Then he turned around. And saw her. His expression was one of genuine surprise. He waved at her. Kashvi walked up to him.

'Don't tell me you are trying on women's dresses?' she told him spitefully.

Nihit stared at her for a few seconds and then laughed out loud.

'I love your sense of humor.'

'Really? I'm glad to know that. So, what are you doing here by the ladies' trial room?' Kashvi remarked.

'My sister is inside. She is a crazy shopaholic and never spares me,' Nihit said.

'What's her name?'

'Erina.'

Kashvi's gut feeling was that Nihit was lying. She waited.

'You want to go inside?' he asked, pointing towards an empty trial room.

'I will. But I want to meet Erina first,' she said, looking into his eyes trying to figure out if what she had said made him uncomfortable. It didn't.

'So sweet of you.' He was very much at ease.

After a minute and a half, the trial room door opened and Erina came out wearing a yellow dress.

'How am I looking?' she asked Nihit and immediately realized that there was Kashvi alongside him.

'OMG!' Erina's hands flew to her mouth.

'Relax. Just wanted to say hello,' Kashvi said, trying to sound casual.

'Really happy to see you again, ma'am,' Erina said. Kashvi gave her a quick smile and entered the other trial room.

Of all the clothes that she had taken inside for trying, she liked one peach-coloured palazzo. When she approached the billing counter, she noticed that Nihit and Erina were fidgeting with a bag. She quietly stood behind them. Overhearing their conversation, she figured out that they'd misplaced something that Nihit had asked her to keep in her bag. Then she noticed something. Something dangling out of Erina's bag. As she looked closely, Kashvi realized it was an identity card, which read:

Erina Tandon

Intern

The Basu Memorial Multi-Specialty Hospital,

Chanakyapuri, New Delhi.

She swallowed nervously. She didn't know how to react.

8

Kashvi was at home. It was eleven in the night. She'd made herself a large peg of JD with coke. Usually she didn't drink whiskey except when she felt disturbed. She couldn't forget about Erina's identity card. And the questions it had raised in its wake:

Is it just a coincidence that Erina is an intern at the hospital? That Nihit is a fan of mine? That they are members of the same swimming club, golf club? she kept wondering. And the more she wondered, the more she drank. Within half an hour, she was three large pegs down. Parth had texted her saying that he would be late due to an emergency meeting; he had asked her to not wait for him, to have dinner and go to sleep.

Kashvi stood up reeling. Walking gingerly and holding on to the walls for support, she finally managed to reach her bedroom. She hadn't changed yet. She went towards the wardrobe to get her nightdress. She opened it and stood in front of the neatly stacked clothes for a while. She wanted to pull out the dress but the alcohol wasn't letting her move her hands. Summoning all her energy into focusing on the job at hand, she started rummaging inside. Her hand thrashed against a bottle of perfume. She took it out, not able to make sense of what it was. She turned to go towards the bed when she tripped and collapsed on the floor.

It was sunlight that woke her up. She squinted her eyes; Parth was parting the curtains. They had French windows and the entire Gurugram city line was visible in the horizon. She sat up hastily; her head was throbbing mildly.

'What happened to you last night?' Parth asked.

'Why?'

'I found you on the floor.'

She had flashes of herself stumbling inside the room and collapsing with a bottle in her hands. She remembered it vaguely. Instinctively, she sniffed her hands. They did smell of a perfume.

'Did you find anything beside me?' she asked.

Parth thought for a bit and said, 'Yeah, some perfume.'

But I never keep my perfumes there, she thought. The fragrance wasn't of a brand she had ever used. She looked at Parth, who was now standing in the balcony outside smoking and sipping black coffee—a regular habit in the morning before he headed to the washroom to freshen up.

That morning Kashvi didn't take a bath. After Parth went to the hospital, she too left. After a long time, she was going to give him a surprise visit at his workplace. And check whether her womanly instinct was right or wrong.

Kashvi was greeted by everyone at the hospital. But instead of going to Parth's cabin on the top floor, she decided to talk to the receptionist.

'Have you heard of anyone called Erina here?'

'Erina Tandon? Yes, ma'am,' the receptionist answered after checking a list on her computer.

'What does she do here?'

'She is an intern with the in-house dietitian.'

'Could you call her here for me?'

'Sure, ma'am.'

A minute later, Erina arrived.

'I didn't believe it when I heard you were calling me,' Erina said, rushing up to her the moment she stepped out of the elevator. The first thing that Kashvi did, as unassumingly as she could, was to sniff her while giving her a hug. It took Erina by surprise but by the time the hug broke, Kashvi knew it was the same perfume she had found in the wardrobe the previous night. Her mind went numb with the realization. She made some small talk and then went to meet Parth. For the first time since she had got married, her husband's words and actions seemed questionable. Suspicion, however minute, is a weird thing. It clouds one's thoughts and perceptions. And this could not have been a coincidence. She did ask Parth about the perfume, but he said that he had assumed it to be hers. Since the bottle had broken, he had asked the servant to throw it out.

While being driven back from the hospital, Kashvi had a bad feeling, her guts were churning. *Was her husband having an extramarital affair? Kashvi Khandelwal's husband was having an affair? The same Kashvi Khandelwal who was on her way to win the 'best couple ever' tag on Facebook? The same Kashvi Khandelwal who was infamous for ditching boys in college? The woman who was hailed as Sita—the perfect wife—on Instagram? You've got to be kidding!* She couldn't believe it.

And because she was in denial, she couldn't confront Parth. *What if it's really not true? What would he think of me?* But then she kept thinking: *could there really be so many coincidences?*

Her phone buzzed with an incoming message. She'd saved the number days ago but this was the first time she had received a WhatsApp message from it.

No post since the last thirty-five hours? Never happened before. All okay? It was Nihit.

Everything was okay, right? she wondered and responded: *Yes. Just down with flu. Thanks for asking.*

Get well soon, he replied. The message made her realize that she missed putting up posts. This too, like her suspicions regarding Parth, had happened for the first time. The moment she reached home, she asked the cook to make some kadha. She washed off her makeup and when the kadha was ready, took a selfie stating: *falling sick sucks!* The comments that followed took care of the mini-depression she had been in since she had met Erina.

It was while she was in her Jacuzzi sipping wine that she heard her help knocking on the bathroom door.

'Madam, Sanisha ma'am and Dhrithi ma'am are here.'

Kashvi frowned. She checked the time on her phone. What were they doing here? Even though she didn't want to, Kashvi got up saying, 'Yeah, I'll be there in five minutes.'

It didn't take her long to figure out the purpose behind their visit. Dhrithi must have seen her 'sick' selfie and thought of coming over along with Sanisha.

'How are you feeling, bae?' Dhrithi asked.

'Much better,' Kashvi played along. Attention was something she never got tired of.

'You could have told us,' Sanisha said.

'It's okay. You people have work and all.'

'Oh, come on!'

Kashvi ushered the women out to the living room balcony. While Dhrithi and Kashvi settled for wine, Sanisha went for a beer. They chatted for some time after which Kashvi said she wanted to ask them something. The other two looked at her curiously.

'A friend of mine told me this morning that she is suspecting her husband of having an affair. She asked for advice. But I am clueless. You know how I can never think of experiencing such a situation, right? So, I wanted to know, what are your takes on it?'

'I think she should catch that husband of hers by his balls and ask him straightaway if he has been cheating on her or not,' Dhrithi said.

'What makes you think he would confess to it?' Sanisha was quick to counter. She looked at Kashvi and said, 'Do they have kids? How sure is this friend of yours about the affair? Is it a deeply emotional affair or a casual sexual one?'

Kashvi went pale for a few seconds. She had thought of nothing of that sort. All she had thought of was how she would face the world if Parth was really having an affair with Erina.

'She doesn't know much about it yet. She just has a hunch.'

'Well, then for starters she should be sure first,' Dhrithi filled her wine glass for the second time.

'I agree,' Sanisha said, sipping her beer. 'How is the woman?' she asked.

'The other woman?' Kashvi thought for a few seconds and then said, 'I'm better.'

Sanisha raised her eyebrow.

'I mean she is better. My friend.' Kashvi quickly corrected herself and added, 'It's been a few years since they got married. She is still sexy enough.'

'Sexy enough?' Sanisha was done with her beer. She kept the bottle on the table in front and said, 'I had read somewhere that the possibility of tasting a new pussy is always alluring to men.' She opened another bottle of beer and said, 'How is their sex life?'

'Okay-ish,' Kashvi's throat had gone dry hearing the 'new pussy' thing. She sipped a little wine and said, 'I mean as much as I know.'

'Spice it up. You know what all Adhik and I do, right?' Sanisha said.

'You guys are extreme!' Dhrithi told Sanisha. To Kashvi she said, 'Maybe she should get impregnated by him and get him back to his domestic life. At least a baby will underline the fact that he is someone's husband.'

Dhrithi and Sanisha kept debating among themselves while Kashvi took in their words. They left after an hour, wishing Kashvi a quick recovery. She then called up Parth, who told her he would be late that night as well. She was craving to know if Erina was in the hospital too. She called up the receptionist.

47

'Ma'am, she has night shifts these days.'

'All right. Keep this between you and me,' Kashvi said and cut the call, feeling sick. She was about to lie down for some time when the doorbell rang. *Who can it be at this hour?* she thought. The help had left for the night. She opened the door and found a little puppy outside with a ribbon tied around its neck.

'Aww . . .' she said. As she knelt, patting it, she heard a click. She looked up to find Nihit standing in front of her.

'What are you doing here, Nihit?' Kashvi asked, while picking up the puppy.

'I couldn't bear that last selfie of yours on Instagram. You don't look good when you're morose. Look at this.' Nihit showed the picture he had clicked on his phone. Kashvi, too flummoxed to think clearly, glanced at the picture. The click had been timed to perfection. Right when the first glimpse of a smile had appeared on her face on seeing the puppy.

'You should always smile, Kashvi,' he said. He WhatsApped the photo to her saying, 'Please make this your next post.'

'Thanks, Nihit, but I can't accept this,' she said, trying to hand over the puppy to him.

'But that's from Parth. Only the photo is from my side.'

'Parth?'

'Yes. He told me to gift it to you when he learnt that I dealt with animals and all.'

'You do?'

'Of course. Side business. I'll take your leave now,' he said.

It was clear, Kashvi thought, *that Nihit didn't know about his sister and Parth. Else he wouldn't have done Parth this favour. No brother can be comfortable with his sister having an affair with a married man,* Kashvi concluded.

A couple of hours later when Parth came back home, Kashvi opened the door with the puppy in her hands; she'd already named it Puchki Pie.

'Thank you for this, Parth,' she said, giving him a peck on his cheek. He kissed her back.

'Thank Nihit. He told me you wanted a puppy and that he could arrange for one if I didn't have any problem. I was like: why should I have a problem if he takes all the headache.'

What the heck! And he told me it was you who . . . was all she could think of.

'Anyway, I'm so damn hungry. Let me eat first, then I'll change,' Parth said. And for the umpteenth time, Kashvi didn't know what to make of this man: Nihit Tandon.

9

Why did you lie to me? The puppy was your idea, not Parth's. Kashvi messaged Nihit the next morning after Parth had left for work. She was sitting on the swing in the living room, while Puchki Pie was sleeping on the floor.

A lie that makes a person smile is worth it. Don't you think? The response was quick. Kashvi was framing her next message when another popped up.

Did you see how many people showed their love to that picture of yours?

Nihit was right. Kashvi had uploaded the picture he had clicked last night on Instagram. It had fetched 80 per cent more likes than her previous three posts. And the comments were to die for. She chose not to respond to Nihit. Instead she checked her profile; Dhrithi had liked the picture as well. Kashvi tapped on the latter's profile and frowned seeing Dhrithi's last few posts. They were exquisite and looked like they had been taken by a professional. She had gone on some trek; the selfies were hers all right. But . . . she called her up immediately.

'Hey, did you get some professional to shoot your pictures?'

'What? No. Why would I get a professional?'

'No, I mean, they are really,' Kashvi's tongue burnt as she said, 'really good.'

'Thanks, bae. The camera has been kind. So, what's up?'

They indulged in some small talk till Dhrithi asked, 'So, is your friend doing anything naughty with her husband? Any spice? You know how much I love listening to all these stories.'

'I'll have to talk to her. I haven't for the past few days,' Kashvi sounded conclusive about the matter.

'Keep me updated on this, bae.'

Spice . . . Kashvi wondered about the word. Some words aren't just what they mean. They are also doors to private confessions that one can make only to oneself. She didn't know if she was born this way, but a Gucci, Versace or Michael Kors gave her a stronger orgasm than the thought of vaginal sex. With Parth, sex wasn't the most exciting activity. They had it once a month, when he would suddenly start kissing her, leading to a five-minute-long fuck. After which he would fall asleep while she would take a bath, pleasure herself and retire to bed.

But if Kashvi was honest to herself, she had never experienced what others, especially Sanisha, often claimed to have: toe-curling, stomach-churning, mind-numbing and hip bone-aching sex. She'd had boyfriends in college but she had sex for the first time with Parth. She was like that businessman who had a lot of money but was waiting for that one investment where the return would not only be the highest but also the most assured. Parth was that investment for her. But even when she allowed Parth to penetrate her, she wasn't the kind who surrendered sexually to whatever her husband demanded. The problem was she was too aware of her nudity. While Parth wanted to make love with at least a dim light on, if not all the lights, she wanted it to be done in total darkness. She was neither interested in seeing herself nor him naked. Parth had no choice but to accept it. And that was not all. She told him straight up during their honeymoon that she wouldn't try the doggy position, which for some reason she knew sounded exciting to Parth.

'I don't like the thought of you staring at my bare ass while I'm on all fours. It's so demeaning,' she'd said. Parth did argue but his case wasn't strong enough. So, it was always missionary and sometimes spooning. And if, only if, Parth could sustain his erection for longer than five minutes, she was okay riding him.

The final blow was when Kashvi told him, on their first night together, that she would never give him a blow job.

'Eww! I don't even know how girls can suck that!' she'd exclaimed with disgust. Parth didn't know what to do or where to look. And now when she was wondering what she could do to spice up their sex life, there was only thing that came to her mind. She went and shopped for some love candles that she thought they would need after they were done. Nothing, according to her, could beat the feeling of relaxing together in a Jacuzzi, sipping her favourite wine. And perhaps Parth would order an exquisite diamond ring online from her tab.

When Parth came home that night, he was taken aback to find Kashvi all dolled up in a red, silky kimono that they'd bought at the Dubai Shopping Festival last year. And whenever she had worn it, the help had been let off early. That night was no different.

'What's up?' he asked, stepping in. She closed the door, held him by the shirt and took him to the bedroom. She pushed him on to the bed. Parth sat with a thud.

'Tonight will be special for you,' she said.

'Okay.' he swallowed nervously.

'I'm going to suck your dick!' she declared, knowing that she could have said it more sexily but glad that she had managed to say it at all. Parth's jaws fell open. Till then he'd only jerked off thinking about the act. Kashvi could tell he was already hard by looking at the bulge in his trousers. She knelt and placed her hands on his already parted legs, took a deep breath and started unzipping his pants. And then she stopped.

'What happened, baby?' Parth asked raspily.

Kashvi had sniffed the same perfume on his trousers, especially near his groin. She stood up.

'Why do your trousers smell of a women's perfume?' she asked, enraged.

'What?' Parth sounded confused.

'It is stinking of a women's perfume!'

'I don't know what you are saying but please can we discuss this after the blow job?' Parth pleaded.

'No! I want to know. Which brand of perfume did you throw in the garbage that night, Parth?'

Parth stood up, irritated and pained at the same time. He took her hand and put it over his hard penis.

53

'I'm fucking hard right now, baby. Please suck me. We can talk after this. I swear we will talk all night.'

'Don't change the topic. You can sniff your trousers yourself.' Kashvi yanked her hand free from his grip. Sex was the last thing on her mind right then.

'Seriously? You want me to sniff my own groin? Oh, why don't you just tell me you only wanted to tease me!' Parth said and, trying to press his erect penis between his legs, went inside the bathroom. He locked himself in.

'Open the door, damn it!' Kashvi banged on it a few times.

A few seconds later, Parth yelled, 'Sanisha and Dhrithi even suck and lick balls. In fact, Sanisha deep throats Adhik. And look at us!'

'How do you know?' Kashvi yelled back at him.

'Men also talk, okay? They fucking brag and I only make up stories.'

Just like I make up stories in front of my girl gang, she thought and said, 'Maybe they too are making up stories.'

Parth opened the door, threw all the love candles out and hollered, 'I would have liked it if you had given me a chance to not make up any stories about our blow job session.'

'What about that perfume?'

'I don't know anything about any perfume!'

'Are you sure you aren't making up any story, Parth?'

He gave her a long, hard stare and then did something he had never done before. He shut the bathroom door on her face. Hot tears sprang out of Kashvi's eyes. She took her phone and dashed to the guest bedroom where she'd locked up the puppy. She cried for a long time with Puchkie Pie sitting next to her. Parth didn't come to console her like he usually did even when she was in the wrong. She needed to vent.

Is a blow job the only important thing? She thought she'd texted it to Sanisha but such was her state that she accidentally sent it to Nihit.

'Shit, shit, shit!' she said and deleted the message immediately. She didn't know that by then Nihit had already read it.

'What happened? Why are you smiling?' Erina asked. She was with Nihit on the bed in his flat. Stark naked.

'First Kashvi asks if a blow job is important or not and then she deletes the message.'

'May I answer that?' Erina had an evil twinkle in her eyes.

'I'm not stopping you,' Nihit said smirking. Erina stood up, walked to a table nearby, picked up a deodorant bottle and came back to bed. She sprayed it on Nihit's balls first and then on his penis from the shaft upwards till the tip. She watched amused as his penis grew for the third time that night.

'It's fucking important! And I like it more when it smells this good,' she said, sucking her cheeks slightly in and going down on him.

10

The following week Kashvi and Parth avoided each other as much as possible and talked as little as they could. This was, as they had feared, their first big fight since they had met each other. Kashvi was convinced she wasn't guilty. His trousers did smell of Erina's perfume; it was the same perfume she had found in the wardrobe amongst his clothes; the same one that he had thrown away. How long would he deny it? What upset Kashvi was Parth's refusal to confront her. It infuriated her that he had tried to steer everything towards her incapability and unwillingness to give him a blow job.

Dhrithi kept asking her about her 'friend' and whether her husband had come clean to her or not. But Kashvi knew that if she told her anything else, she would guess that she had made up the story about her friend. And Kashvi wasn't the sort who liked to be considered a victim. She could never be the victim. She skipped her swimming classes, her spa appointments and her new power yoga class; she didn't even post on Instagram. There was a barrage of messages from her followers asking if she was all right. She enjoyed the fact that people were missing her. But what about her husband? There were moments when she wanted to tell Nihit that his sister and Parth were having an affair, but she didn't. Somehow she couldn't stomach the fact that Parth had chosen someone else over her. She prayed for Parth to confess about the affair and seek her forgiveness. What Kashvi was good at was forgiving others since it gave her a sense of superiority. She knew forgiving a husband who was having an extramarital affair wouldn't mean that he won't stray again, but she was also confident that once she forgave Parth, he would be obliged to remain faithful to her. The waiting continued for another one week, till she came across an article in her favourite magazine titled: 'How to Win Back Your Cheating Partner Without Catching Him?'

The article went on to claim that reverse psychology was best at winning back a straying partner without creating a ruckus and washing one's dirty linen in public. The most vulnerable thing, it said, about human beings was that they could be made to feel guilty. And that's when one could gain control over them. It asked people who were certain of their partner's infidelity to pamper them and make them feel that it was stupid to have strayed. Not only would unfaithful partners ditch their lovers but also display a renewed interest in their spouses. One of the points said 'plan a surprise holiday' for your partner. This sounded plausible to Kashvi. After surfing on the Internet for a good two hours for the best romantic destinations, she decided to head to the Andamans. It would be their second honeymoon. She immediately went to her wardrobe, took out a hooded sweatshirt, wore it, clicked a selfie and posted it on Instagram with a note: *WIP. . . Wife Is Planning. Watch out!* Later, while enjoying a hot bath in the

Jacuzzi and sipping some wine, she felt orgasmic seeing the comments on that photo.

By the time Parth came home that night she had booked everything from the flights to a sexy beach resort for a five-day stay. When they lay down on the bed, quietly—as they had been doing for the past few days—she WhatsApped the tickets to Parth. His phone buzzed; he checked the message. Then he kept it away, turned to Kashvi and kissed her tight. She held his arm. Truce had been called; the silence between them was finally peaceful.

Their holiday in the Andamans went exactly how she had planned. Kashvi wouldn't let him take any calls for more than two minutes; she too didn't use the phone except for posting pictures of their trip on Instagram. They soaked in the sun, went scuba diving, snorkeling, watched bioluminescence at Havelock Island, parasailed, swam with elephants, and the last two days were only about sex. Kashvi drank a full bottle of wine before giving him a blow job. She did it with such aplomb that she surprised herself. She didn't tell Parth, but she had been watching blow job videos throughout their trip to prepare for the moment. And every time they had sex, she made sure it was without a condom. Parth was amazed because she always insisted on safe sex. This decision only excited him more.

Once they were back at Gurugram, she didn't stumble upon anything suspicious between Parth or found any traces of Erina in his life. Even Nihit didn't remain in touch except for a chance meeting outside the New Delhi airport when Parth and she had come back from the Andamans.

'Hey, Nihit!' It was Parth who spotted him. Nihit was equally surprised. Kashvi had to admit he was looking dapper in denims and an aviator.

'Airports are kind of my second home,' he said.

'Of course! It's been a long time. We should play golf next Sunday,' Parth suggested. Kashvi was trying to figure out if Parth was in any way uncomfortable talking to his mistress' brother. But he displayed no such signs.

'Sure thing. I've been missing it myself,' Nihit said and then took his leave. Parth and Kashvi got into their car and left. What neither of them noticed was that instead of going inside the airport, Nihit got into a car. His heart was beating fast since he hadn't anticipated the chance encounter. *But I performed well*, he told himself and calmed down.

Exactly a month after their trip, Kashvi discovered she was pregnant. She'd used a test strip because she'd missed her periods. She had mixed reactions at first as they hadn't planned it, but then she beamed from ear to ear. She had always led the way amongst her friends. She had sex before her other friends did; she landed a job before anyone else; she got married before the others; and now she was going to be a mother before the rest as well. So far, for her Instagram followers, she was the perfect wife and now, it was time to become the perfect mom. Kashvi scheduled a meeting with a leading gynaecologist in the city the next day. The news was confirmed. She relayed it to her parents and her in-laws but asked them to keep it a secret from Parth. While going back home from the clinic, she made a new Instagram profile with the username @celebbaby. She told herself she would name the profile once she had given birth.

Sanisha and Dhrithi dropped in at home after Kashvi shared the news on their WhatsApp group. Kashvi took the opportunity to suggest to Dhrithi that she should consider having a baby as well. Sanisha, she knew, was yet to get married to Adhik. When she broke the news to Parth, he was quiet for a few seconds and then hugged her tight. She was glad she had planned the trip. It gave her back the husband who had drifted away from her.

The next few days flew past with calls from relatives. Nihit came in with flowers after he met Parth and the team at the golf club on Sunday and got to know the news. He paid another visit to the penthouse later to gift Kashvi exotic flowers.

'A would-be mother should be surrounded by what she loves the most,' he said as he guided the men to plant the sapling in a pot in their balcony garden.

A fortnight later Kashvi visited her doctor for an unscheduled check-up. She had bled heavily for the last two days and was extremely worried.

'Did you fall or hit a bumper or something?' the doctor asked.

'No.' Kashvi had a bad feeling about it. The doctor was quiet.

'What happened?' Kashvi insisted.

After a pause, the doctor said, 'I'm sorry but it seems you have had a miscarriage.'

* * *

Couple Talks

'Happiness is when you are in charge of things,' Ashvamedha mimicked Kashvi and laughed. 'Now she'll know nobody is ever in charge of anything.' He was checking a few exam papers at his study table under the light of a table lamp.

'Except for one's virtues. That one should always be in charge of,' Sama said, holding a book.

'Doesn't the tug of war between virtue and vice decide how much one can be happy in life?' Ashvamedha asked, looking at Sama.

'It depends on how thick the line is between virtue and vice for someone,' Sama replied.

'True. You know the best thing about human beings? Doesn't matter what we do, but we always—sooner or later—justify our act. Ask a killer if he is at fault and he will tell you ten reasons why he thinks his decision was entirely natural for someone in his situation. Ideally, Kashvi should have discussed the affair with Parth. But I told you that she wouldn't. And she didn't. For her, the relationship with her husband isn't as important as what it has given her in life. She probably thought that she was saving the relationship by not saying anything. Bullshit!'

'Are you saying if we define life linearly, then it is about setting up a pseudo definition of what's happiness for ourselves and then manipulating everything that comes in the way—and justifying all our manipulative acts as necessities—to live out that definition as the truth?' Sama asked.

'Yes, that's what I'm saying but not many will understand because our own selves don't let us see our acts objectively. We are all heroes in our own stories. Or we continuously aim to turn ourselves into heroes in some way or another.' Ashvamedha stretched himself and stood up, pushing back his chair. He went to the attached modular kitchen and put a pan of milk on the stove. He added a squashed ginger and tea to the boiling milk.

'So, what do you think Kashvi will do now?' Sama asked.

'I don't think she will be quiet any more.' The tea was ready. He filtered it into two cups and said, 'Again, not because her relationship with her husband is threatened but because the position that she has reached in her life because of Parth is in danger. Just consider her case: a girl who was always a gold-digger, an attention-seeker, a hedonist, who wanted to live a lavish life that was not even earned by her, suddenly realizes everyone would be sympathetic towards her. No, I don't think she will be quiet this time. For sure.' He handed a cup of the milky ginger tea to Sama.

'I guess you are right. By the way, nobody can beat you at ginger tea,' Sama said, sipping the tea.

'Thanks. Just like nobody can beat you at being the best partner ever.'

'One of those things you say . . .'

'I mean what I say,' he said and sipped his tea, closing his eyes. After some time, he looked at Sama and said, 'Let me ask you this: all of us at some point in our lives think that whatever we have achieved is made of concrete. It can't be easily demolished until there comes a moment when we realize we tricked ourselves. We only made a house of cards that can be blown away by the slightest breeze. What do we call that delusion? You have only one chance to answer it right.'

'Happiness?' Sama guessed.

Ashvamedha winked at her approvingly.

11

Kashvi couldn't remember the last time she had felt so numb. The doctor was scribbling something on a prescription pad, but for Kashvi, it was all a bad dream.

'Just take this blood test today itself,' the doctor's words jolted Kashvi back to reality.

She took the prescription and asked, 'Are you sure?'

The doctor looked at her kindly and said, 'I'm pretty sure. The test is to clarify a doubt of mine. I'll let you know about it once I am sure.'

Kashvi took the blood test but kept the matter to herself. She pretended everything was fine.

The next day when she took her report to the doctor, the latter had only one question:

'Who prescribed you Mifepristone and Misoprostol?'

Kashvi frowned and said, 'I don't know what you are talking about.'

'You've had a medically terminated pregnancy using abortion pills. Who asked you to take them?'

'I've never had them!' Kashvi turned pale on hearing it.

'Any doctor in the family?'

The answer was obvious. Kashvi couldn't think clearly. *Did he drug my food and juices?* She left her gynaecologist, asked her driver to drive to nowhere in particular, then told him to park on a lonely stretch. Then she told him to wait outside. Kashvi cried her heart out sitting inside her Audi. For the first time in her life, she felt that she had been defeated in the most humiliating manner possible. All her nightmares had turned real. She was sure it was Parth who had given her the pills. *He killed his own baby?* she felt nauseated just thinking about it.

Kashvi howled and then decided it was time to confront Parth. She asked her driver to take her to Parth's hospital.

At the hospital, she went straight to Parth's cabin, oblivious of the stares around her—her make-up was smudged, mascara caked on her cheeks. He was in a meeting; Kashvi barged in.

'Where is that bitch?' she screamed at him. Parth gestured to the others to leave the room.

'What are you talking about? And watch your language,' Parth said. He had never heard Kashvi swearing before.

'What am I talking about? Really?' Kashvi scoffed and flung her reports at him. The colour drained from Parth's face as he read the report.

'Oh my God! How did this happen?'

'You tell me. And that bitch of yours—Erina Tandon.'

'Who is Erina?' Parth asked incredulously.

Kashvi stared at him, came around to where he was sitting and picked up the intercom. She dialed the reception.

'Ask Erina to come to Parth's cabin,' she said.

'Ma'am, Erina finished her internship two days ago,' the receptionist answered. Kashvi slammed the phone down and yelled at Parth, 'Perfect! You asked her to leave so I couldn't rip her head off.'

'Will you please tell me what's going on, Kashvi,' Parth asked, getting up and holding her by the shoulders. She shrugged his hands off, saying, 'You killed my baby, Parth. And I'm not going to spare you for this.'

'Are you out of your mind? It wasn't your baby alone. It was mine too. Why would I kill it?'

'Then who else made me take those pills? My gynae told me it's a medical abortion.'

Parth was stunned into silence. Kashvi collapsed into his chair, hot tears rolling down her cheeks.

'You could have told me you were having an affair and didn't want the baby. Why did you have to kill it, Parth? Why?' she sobbed, hysterical.

'I've not done it. Why would I . . .' Before Parth could complete his sentence, Kashvi landed a resounding slap on his cheek and not waiting for a reaction, walked out.

She left it to him to tell the parents about the abortion. But Parth only told his parents about it and even to them he lied that she had had a natural miscarriage. He was yet to answer Kashvi's question. And she'd made it clear that she wasn't going to talk to him if he didn't tell her the truth about his affair with Erina. When even after a week Parth kept repeating himself, saying that he had never had any such affair, Kashvi decided to talk to Nihit.

'It's really nice to meet you after so long,' Nihit smiled. They had met over coffee at Starbucks at Select Citywalk.

'Same here,' she said.

'But what happened to you? No posts. All well?'

Kashvi only answered his questions after the barista called Nihit's name and he brought their order from the counter.

'I was pregnant and Parth killed my baby,' she told him flatly. Nihit stared at her speechless; tears prickled at Kashvi's eyes.

'What are you saying? Why would Parth do that? He is your husband.'

'He is having an affair.' Her voice quivered slightly this time. Nihit looked dumbfounded.

'When he has a wife like you?' He looked as if he couldn't wrap his head around the news. There was a hidden validation in his statement, which Kashvi was latently seeking. She could have hugged Nihit at that moment.

'I know the girl he is having an affair with,' Kashvi said. Before Nihit could ask her who that was, she spat out, 'It's your sister, Erina.'

Nihit was about to sip his coffee. He didn't. He put the cup back on the table.

'Erina?'

She told him everything but Nihit said he didn't know that her internship was over.

'When did you last meet her?' Kashvi asked.

'It's been a few days. We meet during the weekends because of our work and all.'

'Could you ask her to give me some proof of their affair?'

Nihit thought for a moment and then called Erina. She didn't pick up.

'I'll talk to her tonight itself. If all this is true, then . . .' he paused and added, 'This is so wrong. Why would she have a fling with a married man?'

Kashvi remained quiet.

'I'll wait for your call,' she told him. Nihit took his leave. Sitting alone, Kashvi checked her Instagram feed. People were missing her posts. She sighed deeply, ordered two more cups of coffee and named them hubby and wifey. When they were ready, she placed the two cups on the table, clicked a picture and posted it on Instagram with a note: *time for some togetherness*. Then she walked out of Starbucks, her steaming cups of coffee untouched.

At night Nihit called up Kashvi. She was asleep in the guest room with Puchki Pie lying beside her. She picked up the call immediately.

'What did she say?' Kashvi didn't bother with niceties.

'You are right. Parth and Erina are having an affair. He asked her to quit and has kept her at an undisclosed location.'

'Undisclosed location? Why?'

'I don't know. She isn't listening to me. I told her to come see me but she said she would after some time. Right now, she is happy wherever she is; she doesn't want to meet me.'

'And what about the proof?' Kashvi could feel her pulse racing.

'I asked but she cut the call and switched off her phone,' Nihit sounded worried.

'Okay. Thank you, Nihit.'

'Please don't mention it. I'm ashamed that my sister could've done something like this and messed up your life. I'm really sorry on her behalf.'

'It's okay. She is not the only one. My husband is involved as well. I'll talk to you later,' Kashvi cut the call.

Nihit kept staring at the phone.

'What happened?' Erina asked. They were smoking weed on their balcony; there was a lovely breeze outside.

'She wants proof,' Nihit said, taking a drag.

'If Kashvi Khandelwal Basu wants proof, then we will have to give her that,' Erina said and added, 'after all, we are her die-hard fans.'

Nihit stared at her and both burst out laughing.

'So, what next?' Erina asked.

Nihit tapped a few times on his phone, opened a document and showed it to Erina. She read it and then exclaimed, 'Oh, fuck!'

12

'I don't know anything. You will get me that girl, Erina Tandon. I want her in the office in two hours,' Parth yelled at his assistant. Looking at Parth's progressively darkening face, his assistant didn't have the courage to argue further. After coming out of Parth's cabin, she had no idea what to do. This was the second time she had told her boss that she wasn't able to get through to Erina. The latter had only shared one phone number with them and that had been unavailable for some time now. She wasn't staying at the address she had mentioned in the records. The assistant was sure Erina Tandon had absconded. But who would explain it to Parth? And just as she had got herself some black coffee from the hospital canteen, her walkie-talkie sprang to life. It was the reception.

'Erina just called, ma'am,' the receptionist said.

The assistant immediately dialed Erina's number from her phone.

'Erina Tandon?'

'Yes. Who is this?' Erina asked.

'This is Shefali, Parth sir's assistant.'

'Oh, Shefali ma'am. What's up?'

'What's up with you? Your phone wasn't reachable. You aren't staying at the address registered with us.'

'Sorry. I wasn't well. And I've shifted. What happened?'

'Parth sir wants to meet you ASAP.'

'Okay, I will be right there,' Erina said and cut the call. Shefali called up Parth and told him that Erina was on her way. Parth texted Kashvi: *be here in office in an hour. Erina is also coming.* He sent the message hoping he would sort out this misunderstanding once and for all. He couldn't have been more wrong.

When Kashvi entered Parth's cabin a couple of hours later, she saw Erina already sitting there. She stood up.

'Hi, Kashvi ma'am,' Erina said. Kashvi wanted to pull her hair, scratch her face and spit on her. *This was the woman because of whom her husband had made her undergo a medical abortion without her knowledge*, she thought, and ignored Erina's greeting.

'Thanks for giving me this chance, Kashvi,' Parth said, sounding amicable. He looked at Erina and asked, 'Erina, are we having an affair?'

'Of course not, sir,' Erina responded. Kashvi looked at Parth and then at her.

'Have I ever sent you messages or proposed to take you out or anything that might have suggested that I was interested in you?' Parth asked. It seemed he had rehearsed his questions before.

'No. I won't even think of you that way. In fact, you and I've never met outside this cabin,' Erina said, looking at Kashvi.

71

'Thanks, Erina. You may go now,' Parth said. Erina left. Parth stood up and walked over to where Kashvi was sitting.

'Look, Kashvi, I will never cheat on you, baby. I love you. You know that?' Parth said softly.

Kashvi looked at him for some time and said, 'Isn't it possible that you just asked Erina to lie to me so I would calm down?'

Parth's face hardened immediately.

'Have you lost it?'

'I have lost my baby, Parth. And if you think I have lost it, then so be it. This proved nothing,' she said and walked out of his cabin as unsettled as she was when she had come in.

Kashvi went to Farzi Café in Cyber Hub. Nihit was waiting for her there.

'I'm sorry. Erina is neither meeting me nor picking up my calls since last night,' Nihit said the moment Kashvi sat down opposite him.

'I just met her and Parth,' Kashvi said.

'You met Erina? She is still working there? But she told me she quit,' Nihit seemed genuinely surprised.

'She came because Parth had called her. And she said there was nothing going on between them.'

'Then why would she tell me the opposite? Did you believe it?' Nihit asked. Kashvi, her hands shaking, picked up a glass of water.

'Everything all right?' Nihit asked, noticing her discomfort.

'Nothing is all right,' Kashvi said and broke down after placing the glass on the table. Nihit held her hand to calm her down. She grasped it, saying, 'He killed my baby, Nihit. Parth killed my baby.'

Nihit saw the waiters and the other people in the restaurant staring at them. He picked up her glass and said, 'Please drink some water.'

Kashvi became a little more aware of her surroundings. She drank some more water and then excused herself to the washroom. When she came back, after retouching her eye make-up, she found Nihit busy with his phone.

'What happened?' Kashvi sensed something was wrong as she sat down. Nihit quietly passed his phone to her. It was a message:

I don't know what's up with Parth. He made me lie to Kashvi ma'am today. He asked me to tell her there's nothing between us whereas he had promised to marry me soon. I'm feeling so depressed. I don't know what to do. Please don't call me. I don't want to talk to anyone right now.

Kashvi was burning with rage. She checked the sender's name: Erina. She wanted to do something but didn't know what exactly.

That night Parth decided to stay back in the hospital. He had his dinner while watching the news on the television in his cabin. Soon, his phone started buzzing continuously. He was getting one WhatsApp notification after another. He wiped his hands on a napkin and checked his phone. There was a total of thirty-six messages. He unlocked his phone and checked them. They were from an unknown number. He had received images. He downloaded them. And as the images became clearer, he felt sick. They were photographs of Kashvi with someone. A man. The photographs were taken in such a way that he couldn't figure out who the man was. She had met him at different restaurants, the swimming club and at their house as well. They were holding hands in the last picture. He noticed her dress. It was the same one that she had worn to office that day. *All this could only mean one thing*, he thought. The pictures weren't sexual but they did tell him something. Especially the way Kashvi was smiling at the man. At the end of the thirty-sixth image, there was a single sentence. Parth read it with a deepening frown: *And you thought it was your baby Kashvi aborted? LOL.*

All the dots started connecting in the form of an image in Parth's mind. And when the big image was clearer, Parth hated Kashvi like he had never hated her, or for that matter anyone, before. He threw away his phone. All that he could mutter under his breath was: *You. Fucking. Bitch.*

13

Parth couldn't believe that Kashvi, his loving, caring and perfect wife, had pulled off the perfect game on him. It was she who was having an affair. It was she who had got pregnant with someone else's child. It was she who had aborted it. And now it was she who was trying to put the blame on Parth. *But who was the man?* Parth's whole body was shivering with rage when he called up the number from which he had received the images. It was switched off. He texted back to the number: *we should talk. Call back.* But there was no double tick. He left his dinner and headed home.

Kashvi was on a call with her mother pretending that everything was all right. She had not told anybody about her abortion in the family. It was only Parth's family who knew that she had had a miscarriage. She simply couldn't bring herself to share the news with anyone, including Dhrithi or Sanisha. But she knew she would have to. She would not only have to tell people about her abortion but also about her unfaithful husband and his unacceptable behaviour. For the first time, life seemed to be slipping out of her hands. She had never before felt like a spectator in her own life. She was always in charge, dictating her desires to life. The irony was in the morning she had been tagged on Facebook because she ended up winning the 'Best Couple Ever' photo contest. Kashvi wasn't even a tad interested in that any more. When she cut the call, she heard the main door close. Parth must have come home. She was in the guest room with Puchki Pie on the floor. Parth barged in. He looked livid. He tapped on his phone a few times and a series of messages started appearing on her phone. She picked it up and saw the images Parth had sent her.

'Don't lie. And don't give me excuses. Just tell me why you had to do this!' Parth shouted. Puchki Pie stood on its legs, alert, and then scampered out of the room, its tail between its legs.

Nothing made sense to Kashvi as she sifted through the images. She knew who the man in the images was. Nihit Tandon. But . . .

'Who sent you these photos?' she asked, knowing that the question could raise unwanted doubts in Parth's mind.

'Now I know why you'd to abort. It wasn't planned. It wasn't mine.'

'Don't talk like an idiot, Parth,' she said.

'Yeah, sure, I'm the idiot here who never realized that his "perfect" wife was having an affair behind his back . . .' Parth started crying as he continued with his rant, but Kashvi's mind was racing. *Should I tell him this is Nihit in the picture. But I never told Parth I knew Nihit before. It was one of those things that wasn't even important. Even Nihit didn't tell him. That was a professional meeting anyway. And now if I tell Parth about it, would he believe me? But Nihit would tell him that I knew him strictly in professional capacity.* She looked at the last image. She was holding Nihit's hand tightly. She knew she was crying but it wasn't visible in the picture. *How do I explain the holding of hands?* She looked at Parth. His monologue was still on. Of course, he would understand. And then she realized that she hadn't believed him about Erina in the morning. The question wasn't about the proof any more. It was about doubt. And doubt is a funny thing. It lets the mind construct its own context. The husband and wife, Kashvi knew, had been checkmated against each other.

'This man is Nihit,' Kashvi blurted out. Parth went quiet before repeating his name softly—Nihit Tandon—as if he was coming to terms with a revelation. A hush fell over the room; suddenly it was so quiet that they could hear the table clock ticking away.

'Trust me, Parth,' Kashvi said, her eyes blinded with tears, 'I'm not having an affair with him.'

'Then what are you doing meeting him?'

'He was the one who arranged my interview with The Sensations. We met professionally.'

'Then why did you guys meet like strangers when I introduced him to you right here?' Parth didn't sound like he believed a word of what she was telling him.

'Wait. Everything will be clear. I'm sure someone is trying to work us up against each other,' Kashvi said, getting out of bed. Parth was quiet. Kashvi dialed Nihit's number and put the phone on speaker. The call was picked up after a few rings.

'Nihit?' Kashvi said.

The response came after a few speculative seconds. 'Kashvi?'

'Are we having an affair?' Kashvi asked. She was holding the phone up so both of them could hear clearly. While her eyes were glued to the screen, Parth's were on her.

'Affair? Of course not!' Nihit said. A glimmer of hope flickered on Kashvi's face.

'Hi, Nihit, this is Parth. Did you know Kashvi before I introduced you both?'

'Hey, Parth, no. I never met her before. What happened?' Nihit asked. Kashvi's throat went dry.

'What are you saying, Nihit? Didn't you arrange my interview? We met professionally before, right?' Kashvi's voice was brittle. She could sense her marriage, her life and everything she had built with such pride falling apart.

Parth cut the call before Nihit could respond, giving her a long, hard look.

'Stop bullshitting me, Kashvi. There's someone else in the picture,' he hissed at her and left. A moment later, Kashvi heard the main door bang shut.

14

Kashvi's knees felt weak. She slid down to the floor as Puchki Pie came up to her. Drawing her knees up to her chin, she hid her face with her hands. Her body was racked by sobs. A minute later her phone flashed Nihit's name. She picked it up.

'I'm sorry, Kashvi. Erina tried to commit suicide because of Parth. He is misleading her. I'm pretty disturbed. I wanted to get back at your husband. So I lied, assuming it will hurt him. But why was he asking such questions? I hope you aren't hurt. Can we please meet and talk?'

'First thing tomorrow. I'll message you the time and the place,' she said in a choked voice, cut the call and switched off her phone. Nihit was the only one who could prove that she was innocent. She would ask Nihit to bring Erina. The latter would tell the real story and only then would Parth confess. She didn't know when the plan in her mind diffused into nothingness as she fell asleep.

Kashvi woke up hearing a phone call. Seeing her mother's name on the phone, she feared the worst. And she was right. Parth had gone ahead and told her parents about her affair, which was non-existent, and that the child she'd aborted wasn't his. The latter part was a half-truth. And half-truths are very dangerous. As she talked to her mother, Kashvi remembered how she used to be scolded instead of her brother when they were small. Now it was her husband. What saddened her the most was that her parents—her own parents—didn't try to find out her side of the story even once; they believed Parth blindly. And what he told them were a few one-liners: she was having an affair. She got pregnant. She aborted the baby. Now she wanted to pin the abortion on him as well as claim that he was the one who was having an affair. After a two-hour-long one-sided call, her parents said they were flying to Gurugram the very next day to talk to the Basus and sort things out. All Kashvi knew was this one was going to be way dirtier than she had ever imagined. It broke her down further. The so-called perfect wife for her Instagram followers, to whom she was an inspiration, had ultimately turned out to be a disappointment. She got a call from Dhrithi but didn't take it. A message popped up. She thought it would be Dhrithi but it turned out to be Nihit.

When and where are we meeting?

Kashvi was about to reply when she heard the doorbell ring. She expected it to be Parth. It was him. And his parents as well, as their voices reached her. She texted back: *I'll ping you in some time.* She heard her in-laws calling her name. *Like a true mumma's boy, he had leaked it out to everyone*, Kashvi thought, *instead of talking it out like a mature couple first.* A part of her was enraged while another was already sympathizing with her for the impending allegations.

She walked into the living room. Her in-laws were sitting on the couch. So was Parth. The moment he saw her, he got up and stood with his back to her, staring fixedly at the cityline in the horizon.

'Why did you do all this, beta? Parth loves you so much. We love you so much.' It was her father-in-law. If her parents' call was round one of making her feel guilty, this was round two.

'I'm not having any affair, papa,' she said.

'Then who is this man?' Her mother-in-law asked, waving the phone in her face. Kashvi couldn't believe that Parth had shown them the pictures as well.

'We were not in favour of your marriage; our son was marrying outside our community,' her mother-in-law started. Kashvi rolled her eyes knowing what was coming up. And she had to endure it for another hour.

'We've had a talk with your parents. They are flying here tomorrow morning.'

'There's nothing to talk about. She either tells me the name of the man or I want a divorce,' Parth said quietly and went inside the bedroom, closing the door with a bang.

Divorce? Kashvi was amazed how easily he had uttered that forbidden word. She was undergoing the terrible pain of losing her child but nobody—neither her parents nor her husband nor her in-laws—had asked her about it. All they had on their minds was that their daughter, their daughter-in-law, his wife had had an affair. That too supposedly. She remained quiet. Tears were sparkling on her cheeks. After another hour's lecture on morality, her in-laws left along with Parth, who came out ready to go to the hospital.

'We will talk to you once your parents are here,' her mother-in-law said before leaving. For some time Kashvi sat on the couch with a blank mind. Then she messaged Nihit.

A little more than an hour later he met her at a bar close to her place. This time she was a little wary of the people around her. But no one looked suspicious. She ordered LIT for herself while Nihit asked for a beer. The first thing she showed Nihit were the thirty-six images that were sent to Parth.

'Oh God! These are so misleading, just like your Instagram pictures,' he said. Their eyes met momentarily after which Nihit gave the phone back saying, 'I'm sorry once again.'

'My parents are coming tomorrow. Parth's parents will also be there.'

'For?' Nihit asked, noticing how fazed Kashvi seemed. She was taking long gulps of the LIT.

'If I don't tell them the name of the man in the pictures, then Parth will divorce me.'

'That's what the plan is,' Nihit said. Kashvi looked at him incredulously.

'That's why I wanted to meet you,' Nihit continued, 'Erina tried to commit suicide but thank God she is all right now.'

'What is the plan?' Kashvi asked, finishing her drink. She was shivering.

'The plan is,' Nihit gestured to the nearby waiter for a refill and continued, 'Parth wants to divorce you and get Erina into his life.'

This can't happen to Kashvi Khandelwal. No, this can't happen!

'It means maybe he followed us and clicked those pictures and later introduced you to me after he met you at the golf club,' Kashvi said, picking up the next glass of LIT the moment the waiter kept it on the table.

'Chances are.'

Kashvi loved the way the drink pierced down her throat, but it failed to calm her down. She knew she was drunk.

'I never thought he would turn out to be such a bastard,' she said, fuming. Nihit was quiet, as if he was studying her.

'I won't spare him. He wants to divorce me? I won't spare him that easily. I won't.' Her words were drawling slightly. Nihit tapped on the recorder in his phone. Only the last part of the dialogue was required. The rest would be edited out.

'I don't think you should drive back home,' he said as he knew that Kashvi had driven to the café herself.

'Let me drive you home. You should rest and explain everything to your parents tomorrow. I will try my level best to bring Erina there as well.'

'Yeah. Get her there. Let's strip that dog Parth's intentions.' She kept saying the same thing over and over again, abusing her husband. Nihit paid the bill and took her to the parking lot. He drove her home, unlocked the flat using her keys and helped her on to the couch before leaving.

Kashvi woke up with a bad hangover. She pressed her temples, nursing a headache. Her heart was beating fast as if she'd just woken up from a nightmare. She sat up groggily and checked the time on her phone: 7.30 p.m. *I had slept for the whole day!* She got out of the couch. There were thirteen missed calls from Nihit. She called him back.

'What happened, Nihit?' she asked, dreading that some bad news was on its way.

'You told me you didn't want to spare Parth. So . . .'

'So? So what, Nihit?'

'So, I thought of telling you that I helped you with it.'

'Helped me, how?'

'By killing Parth,' Nihit's voice was flat. No emotions.

'Tell me you are kidding. Just tell me it is not true,' Kashvi said, feeling as if someone had pulled her heart out of her mouth at one go.

'Why won't you answer me?'

'Answer what, damn it!' She didn't realize but she was shouting into the phone.

'I have a question,' he said.

'What question?'

'What is happiness for you, Kashvi?'

* * *

15

Dhrithi Vishwanath and Satyam Vishwanath
(March 2018 to October 2018)
Nagai (Fine Dining and Bar)
Sector-29
Gurugram
9.45 p.m.

Throwing the 3L-followers-on-Instagram party and inviting Kashvi and Sanisha was about making a statement for Dhrithi. Just like everything else in her life, it was about proving a point. To herself. To her long-dead father. And to her husband.

Born and brought up in a small town of Andhra Pradesh, Dhrithi spent the first twenty-one years of her life proving a point to her *Nanna*, father, desiring his love, care and attention all the time. Dhrithi had an elder brother. Her mother had died while giving birth to her. Her father's world revolved around his son. All his dreams were pinned on him. Dhrithi, for him, was the husk; her brother, the rice.

Her father bought her brother a new bike when he was sixteen years old. He drove with gusto on to the highway and was killed on the spot after a head-on collision with a truck. Dhrithi could never forget the evening her brother died. Her father came home devastated after burning his son's body. When Dhrithi, then ten years old, offered a hot cup of tea to him, having prepared it for the first time, he slapped her hard. Till today, she didn't know why she was slapped. From that day onwards, Dhrithi was driven by an intense desire to win his love. Overnight, she became a woman taking on multiple roles of a mother, a daughter and a wife but nothing made her father happy. For him, women only had three jobs: to cook for the man of the house, to let the man of the house fuck her when he wanted, and to produce sons to let him leave a legacy. Dhrithi had grown up hearing that good girls didn't study, good girls didn't have dreams, good girls didn't have desires, good girls married early, good girls did this and good girls did that.

She was twenty when alcohol finally made her father succumb to death. A year later, she completed her graduation and shifted to New Delhi. She worked for a few years, saved some money, took a loan from a bank and pursued her MBA in finance from a premier institution. She met her then senior and now husband Satyam at a freshers' party. He was in his last semester, majoring in finance. Their love for numbers, the stock market and travelling made them talk at length during that party. The next day onwards, Satyam and Dhrithi kept betting on which company's stocks would go higher or collapse. Whoever won bought the other a coffee. The stocks dipped but their love graph kept climbing. Sometimes it was Satyam and sometimes it was Dhrithi who treated. Then coffee turned into beer after two months. Beer led them to confess they had a 'thing for each other'. She had sex for the first time with Satyam at a friend's PG a month before she was done with her MBA. Satyam was the only man she had ever been with. Four years after their post-graduation, they got married. Four years since, their love for stock markets and wanderlust was still intact. It was just that they didn't bet any more. The first dark truth about Satyam surfaced after she got married. She realized he was a mirror image of her father. Only that her father had been a loud-mouthed chauvinist, while her husband was a closeted one. He'd never told his parents that Dhrithi was a working woman and earned almost as much as he did.

'They won't get it,' was all that he had come up with. Dhrithi realized that somewhere it pinched him more than anyone else. She never asked him anything directly. But she did wish, many a time, that she had known this before she fell in love with him. Not that she would have rejected Satyam. But perhaps she would have prepared herself for this. For she had realized that one saw a person through a different filter when they were in love with them. One weighed the negatives and the positives differently once in love. Although Satyam was a closeted chauvinist, he never said no to her if she wanted to travel alone or go somewhere. He didn't impose any restrictions on her. It was only when his parents visited from Chennai that he would ask her to wear traditional outfits. But then again, he also didn't let go of any opportunity to discourage her in a passive-aggressive manner from having higher ambitions.

For him, she had already achieved a lot more than an average Indian woman of her age.

Leaving the restaurant, Dhrithi bade Kashvi and Sanisha goodbye and waited for the valet to bring her car. She could afford a driver but she loved driving herself. She was looking for her car to arrive when she heard a girl loudly exclaiming her name behind her.

'Oh my God! Is that you, Dhrithi?' the girl said.

Although Dhrithi was surprised, she didn't make it evident. She nodded.

'Can I please have a selfie? I follow you on Instagram. Big fan,' the girl said. This was the first time someone from her cyber-life had recognized her in the real world. She was excited. They clicked a selfie. The girl thanked her and gave her a visiting card, saying, 'Please don't mind me saying this but I seriously think you can have 3 million followers very easily.'

Dhrithi flashed a smile at her. Meanwhile, her car arrived. She excused herself and got into her Benz. She loved driving on Gurugram roads late at night as much as she hated them during the day. They were just like life. *What* you hated or loved depended on *when* you were experiencing it. When she stopped at a traffic signal, she checked the visiting card the girl had given her. It read:

Ananya Jain
Co-founder

Above her name was written the name of the company:

SOCIAL KEEDA, a social media strategy firm

This was followed by a tag line: *Do you want to rule cyber space? We will tell you how.*

The signal turned green. Dhrithi kept the card inside her bag and drove on. She reached her luxury apartment at Sector 65 within forty minutes. She was hoping Satyam was home. And he was. Sipping his favourite whiskey and watching the stock market report on television. He only had two ways of utilizing the idiot box. Either watch the stock market news with a drink in his hands or sit with the joystick of his PlayStation. Dhrithi, on the other hand, was horny after a long time because she was happy. As if throwing the 3L-followers party wasn't enough, now someone had finally recognized her outdoors like a true celebrity.

She took off her heels and went straight to the bedroom. While crossing the hall, she glanced at Satyam and said, 'In the bedroom in two minutes.' It was an order. And Satyam knew very well what it meant. He felt his blood rushing down to his penis. He switched off the television, gulped down his drink and dashed to the bedroom. He saw what he thought he would. His wife, stark naked, was standing by the wooden wardrobe, which had a full-length mirror. Dhrithi loved watching herself as they made love.

'Be ready. I'll be back in a second,' Dhrithi said and went out of the room. Satyam didn't waste a single second to strip. When Dhrithi came back, she said, 'I'm so happy today.'

'I can see that,' Satyam said, feeling a slight ache in his erect penis.

Dhrithi popped an ice cube into her mouth. She pushed him on to the bed, parted his legs and held his penis. She pushed back the foreskin and thumbed the pee-slit while sticking the ice cube slightly out of her mouth. She then pressed it below his balls. Satyam let out a grunt, closing his eyes. His wife always surprised him sexually. It was hard to believe that she had had no sexual experience before they had met.

'Where the hell did you learn that?' he asked. Dhrithi rolled the cube on his balls. Satyam grabbed her hair. And when he simply couldn't take it any more, he made her sit on him. They smooched hungrily. Dhrithi pushed Satyam and went to the other side of the bed. She loved it when she was hunted in the sexual game. She lay on her tummy. She could see herself in the mirror. And feel his kisses on her back. She wanted him to pull her hair, bite her back as much as possible, spank her and make her beg for a good, exhaustive fuck. But all she felt was, like always, Satyam flipping her, pushing himself inside her and starting to thrust. He came, like always, in the next ten minutes. He lay on her side, panting heavily. Dhrithi, like always, went to the washroom on the pretext of cleaning herself. There had never been a session when they had got intimate and she hadn't wished for her husband to take her in a rough, animalistic manner, but she had never really said so out loud. She wanted him to understand it instinctively, read her body language. Dhrithi was always ready to cooperate but not lead him to it. And by now she was so used to it that she knew what to do next.

Once inside the bathroom, she cleaned herself first. Then she placed her phone upright on the washbasin against the wall in such a way that she could see its screen, but not before muting all media volume. Next, she turned on the shower and sat underneath it, on the cream-coloured ceramic tiles. She held the hand shower close to her vulva. Warm water cascaded down her bare body while a jet of cold water from the hand shower parted her vaginal lips. By then the video she'd saved in her phone a week ago started playing. It was a porn video from her favourite category: rough sex. As the man in the video started fucking the woman, Dhrithi bit her lips, rolled her eyes and started increasing the intensity of the jet of cold water from the hand shower into the vulva. In no time, she let go of the hand shower and gently rubbed herself, while fantasizing about Satyam and herself in the porn video that was playing. The dirty visuals on the phone and the dirtier thoughts in her mind coupled with the warm water helped her reach a crescendo that she expected to have had on the bed with her husband. After her climax, she sat soaking in the reverberations. A successful relationship, she'd come to understand, wasn't about discovering how many things you liked about a person. It was about getting used to not complaining about the irritating habits of your partner. She stood up.

Dhrithi loved taking showers, which irked Satyam but she didn't care. Normally, she spent an hour under the shower, but sometimes on holidays it went up to two hours. She loved watching herself while taking a shower. She followed a lot of nude photography pages on Instagram and clicked herself daily in the bathroom, checked her photos once she was done and then deleted them later. Dhrithi had lived a sexually repressed life for a long time. And for the longest time she had been told by her father that she was an ugly duckling. Now, the ugly duckling had turned into a sexy swan. And every attempt of hers—be it clicking nudes in the bathroom or presenting important financial presentations to high-profile clients—was about making a point to her father. *Look, Nanna, I'm no more that ugly thing that you said I was. Look, I can have men under me as juniors. Look, I earn more than anyone in our family ever did. Look Nanna, people aspire to be like me. Your daughter is a celebrity, an influencer now. Look, Nanna, I am what you never thought I could be.*

She had discovered that she was quite a narcissist when she had worn a skirt for the first time after coming to Delhi at the age of twenty-one and found people staring at her. In her home town, she only used to wear salwar and kameez. She'd given up that life long ago. Now, she only wore ethnic dresses when her in-laws were in town. Feeling comfortable in one's skin—Dhrithi realized—could help someone discover an indomitable self-confidence. She was fixated on her body, her curves, her rich brown skin, her hair, her firm breasts, her full-moon ass and her toned legs. Usually she was the one who received the maximum male attention whenever she, Kashvi and Sanisha went somewhere together.

Once Dhrithi was back in the bedroom, she deleted the nudes. Satyam was fast asleep. Dhrithi lay down beside him and checked the unread messages on her phone. One of them was on Instagram. Someone had tagged her in a story. It was Ananya. Dhrithi checked her Instagram profile. It was a normal one. She checked Kashvi's profile next and didn't like her latest post. She felt the urge to post something before going to sleep. When there was nothing, there was always a throwback picture. She uploaded an earlier picture of her and Satyam when they'd gone for a desert camp last winter with hashtags of 'couple goals', 'the couple that travels together stays together', 'bae fun', 'when hubby is buddy' and 'best couple ever'. The moment it was uploaded, she logged out of her account and logged back in through her husband's account and commented on the picture: *aww, love you, bae.*

16

Dhrithi was the assistant vice president of a private investment bank while Satyam was an associate with an American investment firm. Although their offices were in Cyber City, they never met during work hours or for lunch. They didn't fawn over each other all the time. In fact, they had never known when they got into a relationship. They had never asked each other any direct questions. She believed Satyam when he said he was out with friends. When she said she was out with her friends, he never asked anything. They trusted each other. The best part of their relationship, according to Dhrithi, was that they gave each other plenty of space. If it was a weekend and they were at home, it didn't necessarily mean that they had to spend time together. She could read a book and listen to her favourite music while Satyam could be playing on his PlayStation or watching a Bond or an action movie. Togetherness had a different definition in their dictionary. The realization that the other person was also there at home was infinitely more reassuring than clinging on to them. Their trips were always planned, but on social media, Dhrithi and Satyam would often spontaneously decide to take a trip somewhere. Their cyber profiles were carefully curated to convey a desired image of themselves.

While she was working on her laptop, a message popped up on the messenger from her boss. He told her that their most important client, whom they had been working with for the last ten months, had finally agreed to extend their contract by another 3 years. She called up Satyam and shared the news.

'Congrats,' he said.

'Thanks. I'm so damn happy.'

'Does that mean tonight also you'll be . . .'

Dhrithi laughed.

'That we will have to find out tonight,' she said and cut the call. She wished she could share the news with her father as well. *Look, Nanna, the girl whom you gave no chance, is now flying higher than most men in her industry. She has impressed the most important client in her office.* Her eyes were wet when she saw Kashvi's story on Instagram, saying that something big was about to happen to her. She called her up but got no leads. Although they were friends, Dhrithi and Kashvi were poles apart. They were both hedonists, but Dhrithi was a self-made woman while Kashvi needed her husband to sustain her lifestyle. She knew Parth was like a free credit card for Kashvi with loads of lifelong benefits. It frustrated her how some people got everything on a platter, but then she consoled herself by saying that her story was truly inspirational, which was why she never shared her corporate laurels with Kashvi because she was sure they wouldn't mean anything to her.

It was while driving with her husband to Kitty Su later that evening to celebrate that Dhrithi understood the 'big news' that Kashvi had been talking about. She'd been interviewed by The Sensations and the video had a few thousand likes and had earned Kashvi 10k followers already. She opened her bag and fished out the visiting card that the girl had given her that night. She saved Ananya Jain's number in her phone and WhatsApped her: *Hi, Dhrithi here.*

A reply came a couple of minutes later: *Hi, Dhrithi ma'am, what a pleasant surprise! How are you?*

I'm good. Can we meet tomorrow? I wanted to talk to you about my social media handle.

Oh, sure we can. Where do you want to meet?

Barista, under Tower 2, Cyber Hub, at 11.30 a.m.?

Will be there, ma'am. See you.

It was time for Dhrithi to show Kashvi who the boss was when it came to being a social media queen.

Although Dhrithi was good at dancing, Satyam had two left feet. They were sitting next to each other but Dhrithi was careful not to touch him. He was dead against public displays of affection. Even if she tried to hold his hand, he would brush her away. While Satyam was relishing the starters and sipping his cocktail, Dhrithi was on her phone, checking her social media accounts and occasionally sipping her beer. When Satyam stepped outside for a smoke, she went to the washroom.

Once she'd relieved herself, she heard a couple's voices in the adjoining toilet. She raised her eyebrows as there was a man inside the women's washroom.

'Such an animal you are!' Dhrithi overheard the woman say.

'As if there is any other way of making love,' the man pointed out. The woman moaned loudly.

'No marks, please! I've a husband!' She sounded flirtatious even though she was seemingly complaining.

'I don't give a fuck!' the man said. There was another loud moan.

Dhrithi wondered how sexy it would be to make unabashed love in the washroom with Satyam. The fear of getting caught made her wet. Dhrithi stood up, flushed and came out of the toilet. She washed her hands and was touching up her make-up when the man came out of the toilet. He washed his hands at the basin adjacent to hers. Dhrithi looked at him askance in the mirror. He had a scar on his left eyebrow. Dhrithi found it insanely attractive. There was a love bite as well on his neck, she noticed. He turned to take tissues when their eyes met.

'I'm sorry. I know I'm in the ladies' washroom,' he said. Dhrithi was about to smile when the woman came out saying, 'I should be the one apologizing. I didn't give him an option.'

'Yeah. I wanted to fuck her. And the male washroom was crowded,' the man smirked. Dhrithi was taken aback by the straightforwardness of the statement.

'It's okay,' she mumbled. The man came close to her and extended his hand to pull out a few tissues from behind her.

'There's blood on your lips,' Dhrithi said and realized it wasn't her business to have pointed it out. *Was it the beer? Or the man? Or the act?* The man glanced at the mirror, wiped the blood off his lower lip and said, 'Thanks.' Dhrithi left before it could get any more awkward. Satyam was back at the table. They drank till Satyam was sloshed. This was their pact. They would get drunk alternately every time they went out. Tonight, it was her turn to drive back home. So, she had limited herself to one beer. While driving back, Dhrithi couldn't forget those moans, the blood on the man's lower lip, and the scar on his eyebrow. Once they reached home, she helped Satyam into the flat and laid him on the bed. She looked at him for a moment and then climbed on him slowly unbuttoning his shirt. She kissed his neck as he remained still. Then she bit him. Satyam grabbed her and shouted, 'What are you doing?' He pushed her away rudely and turned sideways.

Dhrithi took a deep breath. *Whom was she kidding? This was a bad idea*, she thought. 'I'm sorry. Good night, dear,' she said and went to the washroom, muting all media volume on her phone.

17

Dhrithi spotted Ananya as she waved at her from her seat. She had checked her website, Social Keeda, in the morning and learnt that they had handled quite a few social media influencers. Ananya stood up when she saw Dhrithi come in. They shook hands before sitting down. As soon as they placed their orders, Ananya initiated the conversation.

'If you don't mind, I would love to get to the point,' Ananya said.

'I like it that way as well,' Dhrithi remarked.

'Awesome. You mentioned meeting me about your social media handle.'

'Yeah. I wanted to know if my ambition and your plans can help me get bigger than what I already am.'

'You have over 3L followers on Instagram right now. But with someone as promising as you, we can easily get you to 1M followers within the next 2 months. And 1M is a lot more than what some cricket or film stars have in India.'

'I would like to know more about it. And when you say we, it means . . .'

'It means my business partner and me. I'm sorry there was another client to attend to so . . .'

'That's all right. But can I get 1M in 2 months?' Dhrithi said, feeling excited at the thought.

'You have the appeal, a naturally photogenic face and you have done the first thing right.'

'Which is?'

'You've given yourself a USP. An exclusivity. You post your travel pictures, photos with your husband and project yourselves as an ideal couple that travels together. And it works because that is one of biggest aspirations that we exploit on social media.'

'It does?' Dhrithi's question was rhetorical.

'Everyone wants to lead an amazing life. The ones who can't, live vicariously by following and liking pictures of people who can, generating false expectations from life.'

'Why do you say false expectations?' Dhrithi asked.

'Because no one's life is perfect. In the cyber world, people project an ideal version of themselves, something they themselves are striving towards all the time. But a lot of gullible people fall for these projected ideas hook, line and sinker. May I tell about you a real-life incident?'

'Sure.'

'A Class X girl got depressed after the photo she put up of her new haircut didn't fetch the number of likes she'd expected.'

It was disturbing to hear of a teenage girl getting depressed over something as frivolous as the number of likes, Dhrithi thought, and said, 'Hmm. But I would appreciate it if we don't digress.'

'Sorry. So, first, no more vague photographs. Every photo will be shot by a DSLR, in the most flattering angle. We will have themed photo shoots; your account will be verified followed by collaborations with some brands. And we will create fan club accounts as well.'

'Fan club accounts?'

'One way to increase followers on Instagram, especially those of an influencer, is by multiple postings through different accounts. We will create a few fan clubs of yours and send your pictures to other account-holders who promote other people by tagging their handles. It will expose you to a wider audience. Also, we will prepare a lot of video posts, such as the Music.ly ones that are in vogue right now.'

Dhrithi was already impressed. Their order arrived. Although Ananya went on explaining what her company did, Dhrithi had already made up her mind that she would go for it.

'How much will it cost?' she asked.

'25k is our signing fee. And 50k per month is our retainer fee. It's completely up to you how long you want to work with us depending upon the results. And you don't have to shell out a single penny for the photo shoots, etc.'

'Let's do it then,' Dhrithi said.

'Great! My partner will meet you tomorrow with the contract.'

'I'll give her the cheque tomorrow itself?'

'Sure. By the way, it's him. My partner's name is Kshay Rawat.'

Ananya left soon after. On her way back to office, Dhrithi got an Instagram notification—a man named Kshay Rawat was following her. She tapped on his profile. His bio said he was the co-founder of Social Keeda and a photographer. All his posts were of nude models. She couldn't help but be in awe of the pictures. The photographs were in black and white except for the streaks in the girls' hair. Some had green, some purple, some yellow, some burgundy and some red. A picture that stood out was that of a girl with streaks of green hair biting on the zipper of a pair of jeans. Dhrithi wanted to know how Kshay Rawat looked but there were no photographs of him.

At home in the shower, Dhrithi tried clicking photos of herself as Kshay Rawat's models. The photos weren't professional, obviously, but the results satisfied Dhrithi.

The next day she received a call when she was driving to office.

'Is that Dhrithi?' a man asked in a rich baritone.

'Yeah, who's this?' she answered.

'Hi, this is Kshay Rawat. I'm the co-founder of Social Keeda.'

The name reminded her of all the nude pictures she'd seen. She lost her voice for a moment.

'You there?'

'Yeah, Kshay, tell me,' Dhrithi tried to sound as normal as she could.

'I want to know when we can meet. I've the contract and will also give you a complimentary photo shoot.'

'What's the photo shoot about?' Dhrithi asked. She didn't know why she was getting nervous.

'I went through your profile. You have a gorgeous smile. The way your lips part and accentuate your cheekbones makes your smile very alluring.'

Never before had anyone appreciated her smile the way Kshay had done.

'Thanks. So, will it just be a portrait photo shoot?'

'No. We have an apparel brand willing to collaborate with you along with a florist start-up. So, we will do a combo brand promotion with the photo shoot.'

'Sounds interesting. I've my office from . . .'

'We can do it on the weekend if you like.'

'Great. Saturday morning, eleven-ish?'

'Done. I shall WhatsApp you the address of my studio,' Kshay said and cut the call. A minute later the address was texted to Dhrithi. She saved his number.

She made a number of salon appointments on Friday evening after office. Kashvi wanted to meet up for a drink but Dhrithi declined without telling her the real reason.

On Saturday morning when Dhrithi reached the address, she found it to be a 3BHK flat, with a studio, a make-up room and a changing room. Ananya met her in the living room. Dhrithi signed the contract and gave her a cheque of Rs 25,000. A make-up artist dusted and powdered Dhrithi, after which she was made to wear a skirt, a matching top and heels along with some junk jewellery. It was only after she entered the studio that she met Kshay, who was adjusting the lights. He was the same man whom she had seen in the women's washroom a few weeks ago. She could never have forgotten a face like that.

'Hi, Dhrithi.' They shook hands.

'Hi, Kshay,' she said. It was evident that he had not recognized her. Not that she was hoping he would. But she was sure now. The same scar on the left eyebrow, the same bad-boy vibe. He was wearing a baggy white t-shirt with a deep V-neck, which had exposed a love bite on his chest. Kshay saw her staring at it, but didn't try to ignore it. As if the love bite represented who he was, and he was comfortable with it. Although Dhrithi too had a thing for love bites, she wasn't comfortable with the idea of people seeing them. But then Satyam had never given her love bites. He didn't like to.

Kshay explained what and how he would shoot. Exotic flowers were given to her with which she posed. The shoot went well with Ananya appreciating every shot of hers. But nothing came out of Kshay. For the last shot, he wanted her to kiss a flower, but Dhrithi couldn't get the pose right. Kshay walked up to her and asked, 'If I were a flower, how would you kiss me?' The directness not only caught Dhrithi off guard but also excited her. *I would chew each petal off you.*

'He meant if I were a flower,' Ananya pointed a finger at herself, 'how would you kiss me?' She said this assuming Kshay's question had made Dhrithi uncomfortable.

Dhrithi held Ananya's face and, looking at Kshay, kissed her cheek.

'Exactly! I want this soft a gesture when your lips touch the petal!' Kshay suddenly seemed excited. The shoot went well and it was time to pack up. Dhrithi was told she would be mailed the pictures, and that she could post them one at a time the following week. Although Dhrithi expected Kshay to talk to her as much as Ananya did, he didn't approach her after the shoot. She could see him, talking to Ananya, taking the lights off, checking the pictures in his camera. But not once did he look up at her. No matter one's age, when in love, one often starts behaving like a teenager. Dhrithi desperately wanted Kshay to talk to her, bid her goodbye. But he didn't. She hated him for it. But she loved it nevertheless. She had got what she had wanted for some time now. But only Dhrithi knew, deep inside her heart, that rejection—however unintentional it was—could also be deeply arousing.

While driving back, her mind kept going back to the shoot, from the time she had entered the studio and seen Kshay till the time she had left. Her phone buzzed with a few messages. She checked them while slowing down in front of a red signal.

This is my best shot of yours. I will send the rest soon. It was Kshay's WhatsApp message along with a picture of hers.

Nicely shot, she said in her mind and texted back: *were you going through all the pictures? There is no rush.*

Sure. I've a question for you, Kshay messaged.

What? Dhrithi asked and kept staring at the chat window as his status changed from 'online' to 'typing . . .'

What is happiness for you, Dhrithi? he asked.

Finally, she thought and smiled. *Something that isn't business.* She typed back her answer. And with that she didn't know she had walked right into a trap. A foolproof trap.

Couple Talks

'To do what nobody thinks I can do.'

'What?'

Ashvamedha was sitting on the edge of the bed pressing Sama's feet. She'd been complaining of a foot ache for the past few days. And it had become a ritual for him to massage her legs before they went to sleep at night.

'That's how Dhrithi defines happiness. To do what nobody thinks she can do,' Ashvamedha said, putting the lines in context for Sama.

'That's like giving the remote control of your happiness to someone else. Every time she needs to be happy, she'll have to wait for someone to think she can't do something.'

'Precisely what I was thinking. Such a shallow definition. It just undermines one's self.' Ashvamedha poured some more oil into his palm and applied it on her feet. 'You know I was really hurt when your father said that our relationship wouldn't work out.'

'I was hurt too but I knew why he'd said so. Our worlds are so different—not only are we from two different communities, but our cultures and practices differ too. He had thought that I would have to adapt a lot to make our marriage work,' Sama said.

'Probably he didn't know the power of faith. A lot of people talk about love and what it can do. But I think the power of faith is bigger than that of love.' Sama looked curious so Ashvamedha went on.

'When you said yes to my proposal of spending our lives together; when eventually our families agreed to our marriage, we did it with faith. And faith is always blind. But working towards that faith, being accountable to it, responsible to it, gives it a vision. With your "yes", I felt responsible. I felt that come what may I couldn't let you down. I kept asking myself if I was doing enough to deserve your "yes". Of course, it wasn't just that. It was also an opportunity for me to make our lives more beautiful.' He paused and added, 'Your "yes" turned me into a better human being. And I want to thank you for that.'

Sama kept looking at Ashvamedha.

'Say something,' he said.

'I don't know what to say. I think Allah must have been really happy with me to bring you into my life.'

They looked deeply into each other's eyes.

'Come, let me shampoo your hair today,' he said, breaking the soulful trance, 'you'll feel relaxed.' Ashvamedha was about to get up when Sama held his hand.

'Kiss me like you can't risk me,' she said.

Ashvamedha bent down, rubbed his lips on hers gently and then slowly pursed them close with his.

18

'Good morning, ma'am.'

Dhrithi was surprised to hear Ananya's voice. She checked her phone screen to reconfirm. She'd called up Kshay's number.

'Where's Kshay?' There was an unprecedented sense of ownership in the way she asked the question.

'He is busy with a photo shoot. I have his phone,' Ananya answered.

One of his nude photo shoots? Maybe. Why am I bothered?

'I just saw that my Instagram profile has been verified. I wanted to thank you guys.'

'It's our pleasure. Although, Kshay is responsible for it. Amongst all our clients, he has gotten your account verified the fastest.'

'Then I should thank him personally,' Dhrithi said and realized it had sounded wrong.

'Sure, ma'am,' Ananya didn't sound like she had taken it the wrong way. 'Do look up your name on Instagram and you'll find a few fan clubs that we have set up.'

'My fan clubs?' Dhrithi couldn't hide her excitement.

'We will supply them your pictures from the photo shoot ourselves. It will not only increase your followers and strengthen your Instagram presence, but will also position you as a premier social media influencer.'

Dhrithi was getting the hang of it. Finally, she felt like a celebrity. Somewhere in the cyber world there were people aspiring to be like her. And yet they couldn't be like her. She knew her Nanna and Satyam wouldn't have liked it and would probably have told her that *good girls* didn't become famous. But she had decided not to tell Satyam and to not listen to him if he found out himself. She'd blocked every relative of Satyam's from Instagram a long time ago.

In the weeks that followed, three more photo shoots were arranged by Kshay. Dhrithi was made to collaborate with a few Zomato Gold fine dining restaurants, where the photo shoots were done free of cost. But these photos had the restaurant's logo on them. Dhrithi and Kshay barely spoke to each other but every time she met him, she couldn't help but notice a new love bite either on his neck or chest. Once during a break from a shoot Kshay received a call. Dhrithi happened to glance at his phone screen, which was flashing a number and not a name. But the way Kshay talked to the person, Dhrithi could safely conclude two things: one, it was a girl he was talking to, and two, he knew her. This happened a few more times. The fifth time, she asked him, 'Don't you save people's numbers?' She knew it wasn't her business to ask him something like this but she didn't care.

'I remember my girls by their numbers and not their names,' he said with a straight face. The way he said 'my girls' made Dhrithi gulp nervously. She could imagine how he controlled them, pushed them beyond their sexual boundaries and took them into a dark zone, which they didn't know they had in them.

Satyam was out with Parth and Adhik. Dhrithi was at home, going through a financial report on her laptop while sipping red wine. She was sitting on the couch in hot pants and a spaghetti top, her hair tied into a casual bun. Just then the doorbell rang. She glanced at the wall clock. *It must be the dinner I ordered*, she thought. She went and opened the door. And was surprised out of her wits to see Kshay.

'I'm sure the best part of your flat isn't the threshold,' he said sarcastically. It was clear that he was aware that she wasn't expecting him.

'Come in, but what happened?' she asked, stepping aside and letting Kshay in. He looked around and spotted the wine glass on the coffee table.

'I'm so thirsty,' he said.

'I'll get some water for you,' Dhrithi said.

'Oh, no problem. This one is more tempting.' He finished off her red wine. She kept staring at him, marveling at his audacity.

'I hope you didn't mind,' he said as he made himself comfortable on the couch. 'Nobody's home?' he asked.

'You and I are.'

'Perfect. By the way, may I get another glass of this?' He lifted the wine glass.

'Sure.' Dhrithi went to the small bar at the corner of the living room and poured out some wine in another glass. She knew his eyes were on her. And the same clothes that were comfortable to her minutes ago now made her feel naked. She sat opposite him after he took the glass from her.

'I was passing by and I had to give you a piece of information. So, thought of going the old-school way and sharing it with you face-to-face rather than on the phone.'

There was an amused smile on Dhrithi's face. He wanted to meet her. Period. The rest of it was all an excuse. She knew it.

'So much justification doesn't suit you, don't you think?' she said.

'Then . . .' he drawled a bit and asked, 'what suits me?'

'Come to the point.'

'Okay. So, we have managed to get a collaboration for you with the Neemrana hotel. It's not that far from here. We will drive down there this Saturday, shoot during the day, stay for the night and return on Sunday.'

'I'm in.'

'I thought so.'

Kshay stared at her while gulping down the red wine. The stillness in the flat made Dhrithi feel that this was the most intimate moment they had shared so far, even though they weren't sitting that close to each other. And somehow, the silence was slowly becoming arousing.

'I don't see something which I usually see on you,' she said.

'Care to be specific?'

'No love bites this time.'

Kshay laughed loudly and said, 'So, you noticed.'

'Shut up. You flaunt it.'

'All right, I do. Yeah. The last one was a little timid. Like you.'

'Excuse me?'

'Aren't you timid, Dhrithi?' he asked. The way he changed his pose and then stared back at her while leaning forward seemed as if he was ready to read her mind.

'You think timid women make it to the corporate zenith?'

Kshay seemed lost in his thoughts for some time. She was expecting a comeback but all he said was, 'See you on Saturday. My team and I will pick you up downstairs.'

Kshay left after finishing his drink in a rush. Dhrithi didn't get the closure she was expecting. She felt frustrated. The next minute a message arrived.

We will have a clothing brand as well for the photo shoot so don't worry about the wardrobe.

Dhrithi read it but didn't respond.

On Friday night when she met Kashvi and Sanisha for a girls' night out, she posed a question to them after they were done with the first round of drinks.

'Is it okay to have a husband and a boyfriend?'

Kashvi gave her a scandalized look.

'Depends on why you need one. Is it for sex or for companionship?' Sanisha said.

'A companion? Then what else is the husband for?' Kashvi asked.

'For maintenance,' Sanisha said sarcastically but Kashvi took it as a joke and started laughing.

'I don't know for what, but is it okay or not?' Dhrithi insisted.

'Good girls don't have a boyfriend after marriage,' Kashvi said. Dhrithi gave her a long, hard look. For a trice, she thought Nanna's soul had possessed Kashvi.

'I think it's fine as long as the man isn't single. Any two persons getting into something as edgy as an affair should be on the same page to understand the other's position. Like I don't think a single man would ever be able to understand what a married woman's life is like and that can create unnecessary complications,' Sanisha said.

'I don't think it's fine at all,' Kashvi said. While she went on to argue with Sanisha, Dhrithi knew Sanisha had a point. What if the boyfriend suddenly became possessive? She'd read and watched movies like that. Not that she'd planned anything but she told herself that Kshay was a bad idea before gulping down her drink.

The team reached Neemrana Fort Hotel. The drive had been smooth. Dhrithi did tell Satyam about the photo shoot and wanted him to be there but he was too tired and wanted to rest before going on a biking trip with his friends.

Dhrithi was mesmerized by the beauty of the hotel, which was situated in the lap of the Aravalli Hills. Being a heritage hotel, it took her to a completely different era. They didn't spare any nook and corner while shooting. And after a tiring day, she went for an Ayurvedic spa massage. Kshay did ask her to accompany him for the zip line, but she said no. The way he'd kept touching her every now and then during the shoot had already got her excited. However, the conversation with Kashvi and Sanisha had stayed with her. Kshay was an unknown danger. Although transgression was an alluring idea, her marital status pulled her back to reality. She finally made peace with it. *Nothing's going to happen,* she repeatedly told herself every time Kshay approached her to show her the correct way to pose. There was a time when his fingers brushed against her navel. She didn't know if it was accidental, but it created a lot of chaos in her.

After the massage, Dhrithi retired to her room from where she could see the sunset. After a quiet dinner and a short call with Satyam, she parted the curtains of her room's windows. The sight outside was spectacular. Settlements twinkled in the distance while the dark sky above played the perfect host. Then she looked below to the hotel's swimming pool. No one was there. Dhrithi changed into her bikini, wore a robe on top and went to take a swim.

The water was warm as she slowly immersed herself into it. With swift butterfly strokes, she started to swim. The surrounding openness and the sky above made her feel like she was in the middle of nowhere. Half an hour later as she was getting out of the pool, she heard a splash. Dhrithi turned but saw nobody. She held the aluminium ladder, kept one feet on the first step, and was about to get up when she felt someone behind her. From the corner of her eyes, she knew who it was. Her grasp on the railing hardened. With every passing second, his body pressed closer against hers. She could feel his hardness against her ass. Dhrithi closed her eyes. She could hear her Nanna and Satyam tell her, 'Good girls don't do such things. Slap him. Slap him now!' Dhrithi felt him kiss her shoulders. She turned around and gave a tight slap to Kshay.

19

The slap wasn't for Kshay. He could read it in her eyes. The slap had been Dhrithi's back-up plan if her morals rebelled. 'She did deny him but the man didn't listen.' She too wanted to immerse herself in the moment as much as Kshay. There was a momentary silence. His left hand was still on her waist. She didn't ask him to remove it, he didn't oblige on his own either. Not taking his eyes off her, Kshay slowly put his hand inside her bikini and squeeze her left butt cheek hard. Dhrithi gulped nervously. Kshay took his hand out, scooped up in his arms and got out of the swimming pool. His audacity was her aphrodisiac.

The water from their bodies dripped down, leaving a wet trail behind as Kshay carried her to his room. The door was ajar. *Did he know he would be back with her?* Dhrithi wondered. *Was she that easy?* Kshay kicked the door close with his leg. Dhrithi was about to blabber something when he kissed her. His tongue urged and probed and soon she parted her lips. They kissed passionately as he gently pushed her towards the bed. The urgency between them, the heat of the moment was exactly what Dhrithi had always sought between Satyam and her. And then came the most-coveted thing during sex—the control.

'Don't you dare move your hands,' Kshay commanded, pinning her hands behind her head and looking deep into her eyes. There was an ownership in his eyes. She did as asked, feeling him remove his swim trunks first and then her bikini. They were finally naked. As he started licking her, Dhrithi longed to pull his hair. But obeying him was equally sinful. She grabbed the bedsheet instead. It was only when she couldn't take the pleasure any more that she said raspily, 'Fuck me standing up.'

Kshay put his hands around her and lifted her up. Dhrithi pulled the bedsheet out as he took her to the adjacent wall. While trying to hold on to him properly, she dropped the bedsheet on the ground. But instead of the wall, Kshay pinned her against the full-length mirror next to it. His thrusts were full and hard. They made her zone out of reality.

'Take me to the floor,' she gasped after a few minutes. Kshay held her tightly and took her away from the mirror. Sweat from her body trickled down the mirror. While changing positions, Kshay accidentally hit a glass tumbler that fell on the floor and smashed. Dhrithi thought Kshay must have stepped on one of the pieces but he didn't flinch for a second. The moment he laid her down on the carpeted floor, she again zoned out of reality till she murmured, 'Take me to the washroom.'

Kshay stood up and carried her to the washroom. On the way, he dashed against a chair, which toppled. He positioned her in front of the washbasin. And holding her leg up, thrust her from behind. She tried not to look into the mirror but ended up staring at herself as he fucked her. She wasn't a good girl. She had never been a good girl. Perhaps that's why she had reached where she'd in life. There was not a single twitch of guilt on her face. It amazed her. Minutes later she knew an orgasm was building up inside.

'Anywhere but not here any more,' she said. Kshay took her out of the washroom. There was a nervous energy around him this time. He carried her towards the windows and, pushing her against the glass pane, fucked her relentlessly. She closed her eyes and held the curtains for support. His thrusts became short and rapid, matching her breaths. Dhrithi felt she would be torn apart and disappear into thin air. She sank her teeth into his shoulders. She knew she tasted blood, but didn't stop till they came together. They collapsed on the floor with the curtains in a pool around them. Dhrithi didn't know when they fell asleep. She somehow managed to get up, naked. She looked outside. Dawn was about to break. One look at the room and she sighed. It was a mess. As if someone had been fucked without consent and yet she knew it had been more consensual than anything she'd ever experienced. Finally, she'd had sex the way she had always wanted; the way she'd fantasized innumerable times with Satyam.

Neither of them talked to each other in the morning or during their drive back. Dhrithi knew she was feeling at peace because of the soul-satisfying sex, but tried her best not to make it obvious. She did look at Kshay once or twice but he seemed aloof. *Or was he too trying to pretend like he didn't care,* she wondered. He did flaunt his love bite like always. And she knew that she too had become a part of that list of women whom he remembered by their phone numbers and not names. Or was she different?

Dhrithi took an off from office. So did Satyam after his biking trip. They were at home, mostly working. At night while watching the stock news together, Dhrithi suddenly kissed him. Satyam kissed her back. It reminded Dhrithi of the previous night and she felt wet. Satyam paused the television and they smooched for some time. When she felt Satyam was hard enough, she said, 'Take me to bed.' The way she'd ordered Kshay. Satyam, too, complied. He picked her up in his arms and was about to enter the bedroom when Dhrithi's hand dashed against a photo frame. It fell and broke. Satyam put her down and said, 'What's wrong with you? This one was given by Amma.'

'It's okay, Satyam,' Dhrithi said, putting her hand on his shoulder. She was having trouble focusing on it when her mind was demanding something else.

'It's not okay,' he jerked her hand off.

'We can get another frame like this. The photograph isn't damaged,' she tried to pacify him.

'You just killed the mood,' he said. While he bent down to pick up the shards of glass, tears pricked Dhrithi's eyes. She realized her mistake. She was expecting the right thing from the wrong person. She went to sleep alone in the bedroom not knowing when Satyam joined her.

The result of the Neemrana photo shoot came in the form of 2.5L followers in the next six days. Her photographs had been floated by Ananya not only on her own profile but also via multiple accounts, brand accounts and travel accounts.

And nobody could resist not looking at the dusky beauty that Dhrithi was.

A few days later Dhrithi reached office to find a bouquet of fresh flowers. She guessed they were exotic; they smelled refreshingly sweet. She called up the receptionist to find out who the sender was. She was told a gentleman named Kshay Rawat had requested them to be kept on her table. The receptionist also added that he had been waiting for her in the lobby for the past half an hour. Dhrithi texted Kshay immediately.

Are you in my office lobby?

Yes, came the response.

Why?

I prefer talking face to face.

For a moment, she had goosebumps on her arms. The conversation she had had with Kashvi and Sanisha resounded in her mind. What if Kshay was a possessive psycho? She was in no mood to destroy what she had built and shared with Satyam. She knew next to nothing about Kshay. But that was what was most comforting about him. She had been in her element in that hotel room at Neemrana due to that very reason. Dhrithi's throat went dry. No way was she going to get physically involved with him again. What had happened in the hotel was spontaneous. She had moved on. But one glance at the flowers and she knew he hadn't. It was a sign that that night was just the beginning. Dhrithi finished an entire bottle of water on her desk. Another message came from Kshay: *coming down?* Dhrithi stared at it for some time and then replied: *yes.*

At the lobby, it didn't take her long to locate Kshay. He stood up seeing her.

'I'm sorry I disturbed you here,' he said.

'It's all right. Anything up?' Dhrithi asked. She was finding it difficult to not think about their session.

'Wanted to show you something,' he said with a poker face.

'What?' Dhrithi could feel her throat going dry again. Her gut said she wouldn't be happy seeing whatever he was about to show her. Kshay took his phone and gave it to her. Dhrithi couldn't believe it. It was his Instagram profile.

'I'm sorry I didn't tell you before but I wanted to try an experiment. I wanted to capture raw and uninhibited passion through my lens. My room had a three-camera set-up. And I cut these photographs from the video they captured. This is my best piece of work ever.'

Dhrithi's ears turned warm. She rechecked the six photographs. None of them showed her face. Only her thighs, arms, back and butt were visible. She had always wanted to know how she looked naked in pictures but at that moment she wanted to break the phone in two. He grasped her shaking hands and then took his phone away.

'Why are you looking so nervous? Don't tell me you think I will use the videos to blackmail you?' Dhrithi looked away.

There, he had even said it. Cold sweat trickled down her spine.

'Oh, come on! I'm not a kid or a petty psycho. I know you are married. You have a life of your own. And I'm pretty harmless. I have deleted all the videos, except for these pictures. And they reveal no faces. I hope you trust me on this,' Kshay said.

Dhrithi didn't know what it was: a confession, a joke or a threat.

20

Dhrithi didn't want to but Kashvi coaxed her into saying yes to a drink after office. Sanisha was busy so she couldn't come. Since Kshay had left, she had been unable to focus on work. From a 'comforting nobody', he'd suddenly become a threat. She could have threatened him and filed a complaint but what if he still had the video? What if he leaked it? What if she became an Internet sensation for all the wrong reasons? What would Satyam and his family think of her? What would happen to her career? There were more things she would lose out on than gain if she complained. Dhrithi finally convinced herself that it would be better to trust Kshay but also not indulge him further.

Never before had Kashvi and Dhrithi met and sat more quietly than that evening. Both had ordered their drinks and were somewhat lost.

'Anything wrong?' Kashvi asked.

'I was thinking of asking you the same.' Dhrithi didn't want to divulge anything to Kashvi. Confiding anything in her would be like relaying it to prime-time news.

'How did you manage to get your profile verified?' Kashvi asked.

'Huh?' Dhrithi was so lost that she hadn't heard her.

'The blue tick on your Instagram profile.'

And with that Dhrithi understood why Kashvi had insisted on getting a drink. She had been avoiding answering all Instagram-related questions on the phone so Kashvi wanted to ask her face to face.

'A friend helped me.'

'Can you put me in touch with that friend? Actually, I too need to verify my account. Influencers like me get impersonated a lot you know.'

'I know,' Dhrithi nodded and said, 'I'll get you in touch with him.' *In your dreams*, she completed the sentence in her mind.

While driving back, Dhrithi noticed a few WhatsApp messages from Kshay but didn't respond. The next morning when Ananya called her, Dhrithi patiently heard her lay out the next month's plan.

'We were thinking, Dhrithi ma'am, that we would love to post a few videos of you working out at the gym. We can shoot it with a mobile phone. Gym videos are always a hit, especially of someone with as sexy a figure as yours.'

'Thanks, Ananya, but I think I need a break.'

'Break as in?'

'As in I don't want to retain you for the next month.'

'If it's about money, then we can negotiate . . .'

'It's not. It's just a decision I've made. I'll call you back when I want to get in touch with you.' Ananya was still talking when Dhrithi cut the call. She thought she would get follow-up calls from Kshay but nothing happened. Not that day or in the days that followed.

It was Friday night and she met Satyam at a bar after work. She had wanted to meet him outside. Of late, Satyam had been out almost every other weekend and she too had been busy with the photo shoots. They hadn't gone out together for some time. He ordered his favourite Scotch while she opted for a Breezer. After a couple of drinks, Dhrithi excused herself to the restroom while Satyam got busy ordering food.

In the restroom while putting on some lipstick, she received a notification. It was for some Instagram photo where she had been tagged. Her jaw dropped open when she realized she had been chosen the Insta-influencer of the week by one of the most popular influencer marketing platforms. She immediately reposted it on her profile. As the initial happiness subsided, Dhrithi dashed out of the restroom. She didn't want to share it with Satyam as it would mean nothing to him. She would share it with her girl gang and her followers. But outside the restroom, she froze in her tracks. Kshay was talking to Satyam as if they knew each other. Dhrithi didn't know if she should join them or wait till Kshay left. She decided to wait. It was only after Kshay left that she joined her husband. She desperately wanted to ask him how he knew Kshay. She waited for Satyam to tell her about him but when he didn't, curiosity got the better of her and she said, 'Did you spot a friend here? I saw you were talking to someone when I came out of the restroom.'

Satyam shot an incredulous look at her first and then as if he understood what she meant, said, 'Oh! That's Nihit. I don't know him personally. Played golf with him at the club once.'

Nihit? Who is Nihit? He is Kshay! Dhrithi thought. And then a smile spread on her face. *Of course, he didn't tell Satyam his real name.* She looked around and spotted him sitting in a corner alone with a drink. His eyes were on her. Dhrithi took her phone and sent him a message: *thanks.*

For?

For not telling your real name to Satyam.

I told you I'm harmless.

Now I know.

But I'm not here for Satyam. I'm here for you. You liked the surprise?

Dhrithi read the message twice before realizing what he was talking about.

Thanks again for making me the Insta-influencer of the week.

You're welcome. But I think we need to talk. Been long.

Dhrithi thought for a moment. She felt thrilled at the idea of standing next to her husband and texting a man with whom she had had a one-night stand.

Yeah, I agree, she texted.

Tomorrow night, Hotel Visaya, room number 305?

Listen, I don't want to meet in a hotel room.

There was no response. She looked up. He was staring at her. And then he typed something. Dhrithi opened the chat window before the message came. And when it popped up, she gulped nervously.

Those lips of yours look way juicier without lipstick. Those eyes emanate more fire without make-up. That hair when undone wakes up the animal in me. That body without clothes feels so much like home. You and I are about instincts, Dhrithi.

She ran her fingers through her hair, sat up and finished the Breezer in one go. By then, another message had arrived:

I promise nothing will happen that you don't want. Trust me.

Dhrithi wondered why certain temptations were stronger than any resolutions ever made.

Okay, she replied.

The hotel was in Panchsheel Park in Delhi. She drove there right after office the next day. She was taken to the room by a staff member. When the door opened, she realized it was pitch dark inside. Then something glowed in the dark. It was a face.

'Satyam?' Dhrithi mumbled, shocked.

21

There was pure horror in her voice when she took her husband's name. *How on earth would Satyam be here?* Her mind went blank. Dhrithi wanted to switch on the lights. She turned to look for the switchboard when she heard a man say, 'Relax! Let it be dark. This isn't Satyam.'

Dhrithi knew the voice. It was Kshay.

'Care to explain what's up?' she calmed down a bit.

'When you said no to Ananya the other day, I understood your problem. So, here I am with the solution.'

'What's my problem?' Dhrithi asked. It was weird staring at a glowing face that looked like her husband's. She'd guessed by now what it could be but wanted Kshay to tell her.

'Your problem was fear and guilt. Fear because you think getting involved with me might make me fall for you, which could compromise your marriage. Guilt because what you got from me, you actually want from your husband.'

'What the . . .' Dhrithi knew he was spot on.

'So, here's the solution. I've made a radium mask resembling your husband's face. Well, almost.' Kshay smirked and added, 'You can call me Satyam as well. Neither I nor you are going to tell anyone. Can't it be our little secret, Mrs Good Wife?'

Dhrithi was anything but 'good', nor did she aspire to be one. And now Kshay had broken the walls of fear and guilt she had created to keep him away. Dhrithi started stripping as she saw him wear radium gloves. She could now see something glowing on the bed. It read: fuck me hard. It was a radium sticker, which he'd perhaps kept hidden at first. As she approached him, Kshay pasted the sticker on her as he flipped her and bit her back. He pushed her against a chair in the room and positioned himself behind her, rubbing the tip of his erect penis on her wet vagina. Then he slowly pushed inside. He brought his mouth close to her ears and along with his thrusts, started murmuring in her ear.

'Just immerse yourself in the moment. There's nothing beyond or before. It's just you and me. It's your husband and you.'

Dhrithi had closed her eyes. In her mind, it was Satyam talking.

'You always wanted to be your husband's bitch, isn't it?' Kshay whispered in her ear.

'Yes,' she said, feeling his thrusts hitting the right spot inside her.

'You always wanted him to treat you badly in bed.'

'Yes.'

'Here you go. Live your fantasy, girl,' Kshay said and thrust her harder holding on to her waist for support. Dhrithi twisted around to see a glowing face.

'Fuck me hard, Satyam. Damn, I've been waiting for this for so long.'

'You don't have to wait for it any more. Every time you want it, your husband will give it to you.'

Kshay's thrusts were hitting her G spot, generating unprecedented pleasure. He kept fondling her breasts from behind, flicking her nipples with his thumbs while rubbing his face on her shoulders. He whispered dirty questions into her ear, squeezing out dirtier confessions till she could no longer take it.

'Just hold me, Satyam. I'm going to climax. Now!'

'First, tell me what does happiness mean to you, Dhrithi?'

'This! This! This!' She came. Kshay too came. He held her and helped her on to the bed. Dhrithi lay down, totally sapped of energy. As her breathing became normal, she noticed that even Kshay's condom was glowing.

'I swear I had never thought men could be this kinky. Who are you? The fucking kink-god?'

Kshay laughed as he removed the sticker off her. They didn't talk much but they knew they would continue this nothing-to-lose arrangement. She was so happy she had met Kshay.

Dhrithi reached home to find Satyam hooked to his PlayStation.

'What happened?' he asked.

For a moment Dhrithi thought he had spotted a love bite.

'What?'

'You look happy. In a different way.' Satyam paused his game to get a better look at her. It made her uncomfortable.

'Yeah? Nothing,' she said and excused herself to the bedroom. She immediately went to the washroom and checked herself in the mirror.

Is that what satisfying sex does to you? she wondered, looking at her reflection. She couldn't yet figure out the difference. But she wished Satyam would understand the reason behind it as well. Probably then she wouldn't have to imagine him while doing it with another man. Dhrithi sighed. And she could have been his good girl that he always wanted her to be. Her trance was broken by the sound of a message. It was her boss.

Congrats. Just saw the email where you have been promoted. It will be announced tomorrow.

Dhrithi was so happy that she could have cried. She had worked her ass off for the promotion throughout the year. It seemed that all the stars were shining down on her. She went to tell Satyam about the news.

'There is something I want to tell you,' she said. Satyam raised his eyebrows.

'I got a promotion!' She came and hugged him.

'That's . . . that's awesome. Congrats!' he said. But she could sense that he wasn't very happy. It didn't take her long to understand why. According to him, and men like him, good girls neither earned more than their husbands nor did they have higher designations. Dhrithi now had both.

'Thanks.' She broke the awkward conversation and went to the kitchen to serve dinner for them both.

Back in the hotel, once Dhrithi had left the room promising Kshay she would continue with Social Keeda's services, someone knocked on the door. Kshay opened it to find Ananya. She slapped him hard. Then she stepped inside, banging the door shut behind her.

'What happened?' Kshay said, reeling under the suddenness of the slap.

Another slap. This time harder.

'Will you tell me what happened?'

'Playing brother—sister for Kashvi was all right,' Ananya said, 'but I don't like that you have to fuck Dhrithi. It just breaks me.' She hugged him; her body shuddered. He knew she was crying. His eyes grew moist too and he hugged her back.

'You think I like it?' he asked. He cupped her face in his hands. Tears were rolling down her cheeks. And he couldn't see the love of his life in tears.

'Stop crying. I'm just doing what is good for us. You know that, right?'

Ananya nodded and whimpered, 'I know everything, but . . .'

'Just because I fucked another woman doesn't mean my love for you has been compromised.'

Ananya looked into his eyes and said, 'Our love shall win, right?'

The response came after Kshay looked back at her equally intensely.

'It will. It has to.'

'Let's take a long shower. I want to soap that bitch's fragrance off you,' she said.

'Yes, sure.' The duo headed for the bathroom holding hands.

22

Everyone congratulated her in office once the news was made official. But the irony of Dhrithi's life was that she couldn't share it with anyone. Her in-laws didn't know she was working and she wasn't in touch with her relatives. She did Instagram the screenshot of her promotion email and gained a lot of good wishes from her followers, but she was not sated. She shared the screenshot with Satyam as well on WhatsApp and all that came was a thumbs up and an angel emoji. She understood he wasn't happy with the development. But she understood the extent of his unhappiness only when she retired to bed that night beside him.

'I think it's time,' he said. She frowned. They were lying on their backs staring at the ceiling in the dark.

'Time for?' she asked. Her heart was racing.

'For us to plan a family. Amma has been after my life. I didn't tell you before but now I think . . .' Satyam turned towards her, holding her in his arms, and said, 'Let's become three.'

Why specifically tonight, Satyam, why not before when Amma had said it? Dhrithi felt tempted to ask. She didn't.

He looked at her lovingly but his intentions were what her father had had a long time ago. Her father had wanted another child, hoping that he would get a son. Her husband, likewise, wanted a family not because he wanted a child but because he wanted her to quit working. She knew that once they had had a child, his mother would move in with them. And since his parents didn't know that she was a working woman, she would have to let go of her job, her career, her life to fulfil that lie. Dhrithi wanted to be a mother but not right then. She wondered how women weren't even allowed to decide when they wanted to have a child.

'I've taken an appointment with a renowned gynaecologist. We shall go this weekend. One of my colleagues said it's better to consult a doctor and then start planning,' Satyam said and kissed her lips. He had never tasted more bitter.

'I'm not ready now, Satyam. I need some time.'

'How much time?'

'Like two or three years maybe.'

'"Two or three years?" You'll cross thirty by then. We must have a baby before that and now is the time. Every good and cultured married woman has her baby by thirty.'

Dhrithi wanted to spit on her husband's face.

'But what's the hurry?' Dhrithi sat up, removing his hand from around her.

'Give me one reason why we shouldn't hurry?'

'What about my career?'

'You'll always have your career, so?'

Dhrithi was quiet. She knew it was a trap. He would say it was all right for her to work after having a child. Like he had said that he would eventually tell his family that she was a working woman. But that day hadn't come yet.

'Should I presume you aren't interested?' Satyam asked.

'It's not that. I just got a promotion. I'll have bigger responsibilities and my working hours might also be longer. Let me settle in a bit and . . .'

'Who asked you to get a promotion? Weren't you happy doing what you were? I'm sure you aren't so dumb that you didn't foresee the promotion bringing you bigger responsibilities,' Satyam said.

'Are you saying my promotion is a mistake?'

'All I'm saying is there is a time for one's career and there is a time for starting a family, especially for women.'

The last part made Dhrithi livid. She somehow managed to calm herself down.

'We are planning a family. That's it. Don't challenge this decision of mine. I've already told Amma about it and she was more than happy for us,' Satyam said, turned around and went to sleep.

Dhrithi remained tense the next day. Her only sources of happiness were the comments and messages she got from her followers on the photos she'd put up. Her fan club was also getting a lot of traction. When Kshay called her to ask if she was free to meet up, Dhrithi didn't think twice before saying yes.

They met at his studio. There was nobody there except for them. They hugged once they met. Kshay had started to kiss her when she stopped him saying, 'Not today.'

'Good. Even I'm not in the mood.' Saying so, he went to the kitchen.

'What happened?' she asked, following him.

'Black coffee?' he asked. Dhrithi nodded. It was only when they took their mugs and went outside to the balcony, that Kshay spoke. 'I need some money urgently. There are some bad guys after my life.'

'Oh, care to explain?'

'It's a long story. I need 1.5L by tonight else they will kill me.'

Dhrithi froze. 'Kill you? Are you serious?'

'I told you they were bad people.'

The tense look didn't suit Kshay. It made him way too predictable.

'Did Ananya tell you I'm going to continue with you guys for my social media marketing?'

'Yeah, she did.' Kshay was sipping his coffee looking at the cityline in the distance.

'I can give you the money in advance,' she said with a straight face.

A slow smile spread on Kshay's face. He hugged her tightly, spilling a little coffee.

'What are you doing? I don't like to waste my coffee,' she said jocularly.

'Thanks a lot, Dhrithi,' Kshay said, looking deep into her eyes.

'I'm sure you know how to thank me in kind.' Dhrithi had a naughty smile.

'I sure do.' He gave her a peck. Dhrithi sighed and said, 'I'll transfer you the money when I reach home.'

'That's cool. But what's up with you? I can sense something's wrong at your end as well.'

The mere mention of 'something wrong' made Dhrithi realize how badly she wanted to burst out. She didn't waste a single second to tell Kshay her story. From her father to Satyam and how the only difference between the two was that the former was a proud chauvinist while the latter was a closeted one.

Kshay hugged her tightly after she told him she didn't want to become a mother so soon. Dhrithi held on to him and cried for a long time. Then Kshay whispered a stop-gap idea to her. She couldn't help but give him a peck.

Satyam did take her to the gynaecologist in the weekend. The doctor checked and found that everything was well with Dhrithi. That night after dinner, she had an inkling that Satyam would try. And he did. For the first time in their marriage, they got intimate without using protection. He came inside her. Dhrithi didn't waste a single moment to go and wash herself and then execute Kshay's plan. She took an i-pill. Later, she went on the pill secretly. She needed time to become a mother. If it was not given to her, she would give it to herself, her own way. When she popped the pill, Dhrithi had a victorious smile on her face.

'Don't worry, Nanna, and don't worry, Satyam, you won't ever turn me into a good girl,' she muttered to herself. By the time she back came to bed, Satyam was already asleep. She was surfing her newsfeed when she received a message from Kshay.

Awake?

Yeah, what's up? she responded.

You don't have to give me the money. The night Dhrithi was about to transfer the amount, Kshay had asked her to wait so she had.

What happened?

I had a talk with them. They are willing to wait a little.

That's wonderful.

But thanks nonetheless.

Don't mention it.

I won't but as you said I will thank you in kind.

Ahaan! I'm listening.

He sent an image. It was a flight ticket to Goa. The date was Monday.

What the hell?

I'm taking you to Goa for a day. I've something super kinky planned for us.

But how will I go? I've got office. What would I tell Satyam? What if he calls in between?

You and I are about adventure, Dhrithi, and not excuses.

She smiled reading the message. Another one came up next.

Okay, let me tell you we will be Batman and Catwoman in Goa.

What? What's that supposed to mean?

Just be there at the airport on time. And discover the rest like a true bad girl.

The last two words, *bad girl*, made her high. 'Incorrigible,' she murmured and replied: *All right, see you tomorrow morning then.* She got up and started her packing while planning what she'd tell Satyam. If at all it were needed.

The only thing Dhrithi didn't know was that what would hit her in Goa would shake her whole world.

23

This was something Dhrithi had never thought about. Escaping with another man to a different town without telling her husband or anyone else for that matter. It was one of those things you just did and never thought about. Sitting on the flight beside Kshay, as it took off from New Delhi, she knew she had done it. If Satyam called, which he never did during office hours, when she was flying, she would tell him later that there were connectivity issues. She'd left her car at the New Delhi airport parking lot.

It was a short flight. The ride from the airport to the resort at Ashvem Beach took time but went smoothly. The resort was mainly under construction. It had a restaurant in the front and a few villas for rent behind. Kshay had booked one of the villas. The plan was that he would check in and she would later come in as a visitor.

They went for a stroll on the beach after he checked in. The sun was rich, but she was careful not to carry any possible tan back. They finished a few beers on the beach and headed to their villa for a nice, relaxing shower together. The best part was, Dhrithi realized, that Kshay didn't click any selfies or photos. Whatever photos he had clicked of Dhrithi were all part of their professional deal. Except for the video in the hotel room at Neemrana, Kshay had never mixed business with pleasure. Although she had been shocked when he had told her about the video, she later appreciated the fact that he had been honest about it. Somewhere, she believed he must have deleted the video.

It was after the shower that Kshay told her he had brought costumes for them. He would be Batman and she Catwoman while they had sex. She laughed at the idea of role play but also participated in it excitedly. The Catwoman costume was a body-hugging leather dress and she couldn't help but marvel at her curves. She was itching to click a picture and post it, but knew it might draw Kashvi's attention. And she didn't want any outsider to be a part of this one-day vacation.

The session was one of the most hilarious she had ever had. They made out, but the role play made it funny. Especially when Kshay started talking to her in Christian Bale's voice from *The Dark Knight*. When they were done, she went to the washroom to change. Looking at her reflection in the mirror, she realized this was, perhaps, the most amazing time she had had in a long, long time. She sat down to pee, and was surfing Instagram, when she received a tagging notification. Kshay had tagged her in the Catwoman costume photo. But when did he click her? And why did he tag her? She hid the picture from the tagged photos' section and got out of the washroom. What she saw outside changed her life forever.

24

It was only when Dhrithi's Goa to New Delhi flight took off that she breathed a sigh of relief. The empty seat beside her kept reminding her of the scene in the hotel room—Kshay in a pool of blood. Her first instinct was to scream, call for help, call the police, but then reality hit her like a slap on her face. What would she tell people? Tell the police? Tell Satyam? She was with this man, her social media manager, in a beach resort, wearing a Catwoman costume? She took a few deep breaths and finally decided she wouldn't tell anyone anything. Nobody as such had seen her entering the resort anyway. There was no proof that she had been there. Except that the airlines had her name. But there could have been a thousand Dhrithi Vishwanaths in the world. While all these thoughts kept crowding in her mind, another one swept all of them away. But what if someone had seen her and she didn't know about it? Her eyes were moist as she stared at the clouds overhead and for the first time in her life wished that she had listened to her Nanna, to Satyam. And been a good girl.

Dhrithi left IGI as quickly as possible. Thankfully, there were no missed call alerts or messages from Satyam. It was only when she got into her car that she broke down. She was sure that the people whom Kshay had told her about had killed him. But why did they do it when she was with him? Why did they have to ruin her life? She prayed to never be traced down for his murder. She was itching to call up the resort, but she knew it would be calling for trouble. The police must be there by now, she was sure.

A day later Dhrithi, who was now a little more in control of herself, called up Ananya. She wanted to make sure that Kshay hadn't told her anything about them. If Ananya didn't know, nobody would.

'Hi, Ananya, I've been calling up Kshay since last evening. He isn't taking my calls,' Dhrithi said.

There was a pause, after which she heard Ananya crying.

'What happened?'

'Kshay was murdered in Goa,' Ananya said in a choked voice.

'Murdered? How? What was he doing in Goa?' Dhrithi's shock was rehearsed.

'I don't know what he was doing in Goa. In fact, we didn't have any work there. He was with me in the studio on Sunday evening and then the next evening, I hear he is dead,' Ananya said.

'Oh dear! Okay,' Dhrithi breathed a sigh of relief.

'I'm sorry, Dhrithi ma'am. I think I'll take off for a few weeks and . . .'

'Don't worry, Ananya. I totally understand. And I'm really sorry about Kshay. You take your time and take care,' she said and cut the line. Dhrithi was finally able to concentrate on work.

That weekend while Satyam was away with his friends, she came home after dinner with Kashvi and Sanisha. She took a long shower. While looking at her body, instead of clicking pictures like always, she picked up her phone and looked up Kshay's Instagram profile. But to her surprise, the account seemed to have been deleted. *Perhaps Ananya did it*, she thought. Dhrithi kept the phone away and was drying her hair, when she received a message on her WhatsApp. It was a link from a number she hadn't saved on her phone. She clicked on it. It took her to a YouTube video. The title of the video said it was unpublished. Her heart started racing when she saw the one-minute-long video. It was of the resort room. It showed her coming out of the washroom, finding Kshay in a pool of blood and leaving hurriedly. Dhrithi immediately called up the number. It was switched off. She called it on WhatsApp and was rejected. She messaged back: *who is this? What do you want?*

Another link came up once her messages were read. By then, she understood her deepest fears had come alive. She clicked on the link. It took her to another YouTube video. As she played it, there was only text in it, which read: *there is something inside the dashboard of your car. Go and check now.*

Dhrithi had broken into a cold sweat. She quickly wore a pair of jeans and a top and ran downstairs to the parking. She unlocked her car, looking around for any suspicious person, and opened the dashboard. There was a plastic pouch. She took it out, opened it and then noticed what it had. Three syringes. Loaded with some liquid. She messaged back:

What's this?

Another link. Another YouTube video with text that read:

Don't worry about what this is. You have two options and I have one. First, your options: either you inject these syringes into yourself—one after the other—right now or into your husband when he comes back tonight. If you don't choose either of these two, my only option is to pass the first video to Goa Police the first thing tomorrow morning.

Dhrithi's throat had gone dry. She was having trouble breathing. She got out of the car and ran her fingers through her hair staring at the syringes and then at nothing in particular. Why her? What was in the syringes? How was Kshay's death related to her injecting whatever shit there was in these syringes into herself or Satyam? She called up Ananya. But a mechanical voice told her that her phone was not reachable. Dhrithi stamped her feet on the ground. Tears ran down her cheeks. With unsteady hands, she checked the number on her TrueCaller app. It threw up three words that she was certain wasn't a name.

What is happiness?

What could it possibly mean? It was Dhrithi's last thought as she saw Satyam's name flashing on her phone's screen. She had a feeling that life would never be the same again.

* * *

25

Sanisha Singh and Adhik Sharma
(March 2018 to October 2018)
Nagai (Fine Dining and Bar)
Sector-29
Gurugram
9.45 p.m.

Every time she had a dinner with Kashvi and Dhrithi, Sanisha ended up cursing herself. She had never connected with these two women at any level. And she cringed every time they started talking about their social media celeb status. Sanisha found it all fake. To project an edited truth to everyone and gain a fan following on the basis of that was something Sanisha could never do. Her mantra was simple: I am what I am. Take it or leave it'. She couldn't be a filtered version of herself in the cyber world just because that was the trend. She was active on social media to the extent of being in touch with old school and college friends. Her live-in partner, Adhik, was more social than her. But they never posted each other's pictures.

At twenty-nine, Sanisha was the only girl in her family to still be unmarried. Her parents were based in Bhopal and the average age of marriage of a girl in her family was twenty-two. The Singh family ran a progressive Hindi newspaper called *Kal ka Bharat*, but at home they were appallingly regressive. The men in the family ran the newspaper, while the women were married off early. What made Sanisha different was that she had lived most of her life away from her family. She was a national-level swimmer while she was studying at a boarding school in Dehradun. Her parents were probably the most liberal of all the family members and had hence decided to keep her away. But when Sanisha won a silver medal at a national-level sporting event, her family didn't appreciate her victory. All they saw was that she was wearing a swimsuit and was being telecast on national television. Her grandfather ordered his son to bring her back home and admit her in a school in Bhopal. Sanisha came back from Dehradun after finishing Class X and studied in Bhopal till her graduation. For her post-graduation, she shifted to Delhi. Her father fought for her at home and allowed her to take her own decision. He refused to listen to his brothers and father and get her married.

It was during the second semester of her MBA that she decided to go out with Adhik, who had been pursuing her since her post-graduation days. Till then she didn't know that a person could change our thoughts and perspectives and make us see things in a different light. Although her parents had supported all her decisions so far, Sanisha knew they would never accept her decision to stay with Adhik. So she kept it a secret from them.

Sanisha felt relieved when Kashvi and Dhrithi decided that they were done. While they drove back home, Sanisha booked an Uber. She had a car but rarely drove around in it. Sanisha and Adhik were a FIRE (financial independence to retire early) couple. Even though they could afford a driver, they didn't hire one. They planned to retire by forty and buy a house in Pondicherry. There, they would do organic farming and enjoy a serene life, and go on an annual, budgeted, backpacking holiday. Unlike Adhik who worked at a senior position in a consulting firm, Sanisha worked with an NGO for a comparatively less salary. But the job gave her immense satisfaction.

Five minutes after getting inside the cab, one of her friends, Shweta, from the NGO called her. Her son's annual day had just got over and she was going back home and wanted to know if Sanisha was anywhere around. The latter said that she was nearby and would pick them up. They lived close to each other in Dwarka. Shweta, a single mother, had been Sanisha's friend since her first job. Sanisha changed her drop location and in fifteen minutes reached the school. She met Shweta, who was gung-ho about the fact that her son had won the first prize in three events. They were waiting for another Uber when Sanisha saw someone she thought she knew. A little turn of the head and she was certain. She might already have found the love of her life but this man had been her Mr Perfect. He was neither her crush nor her love. He fell in a grey space within the two that even she couldn't define. Sanisha had spent her MBA days secretly staring at him. Not because he was handsome, but because he was the most honest and courageous man she'd ever known. It had been some years since she'd last seen him.

'What happened? Why are you smiling?' Shweta asked.

Sanisha excused herself and approached the man. He was standing alone, waiting for something, looking left and right.

'Ashvamedha?' she asked. The man turned, took a few seconds before saying, 'Sanisha Singh? How are you?'

She wasn't ready for this serendipitous meeting. Nor was he.

26

'I can't believe this. We are meeting after . . .' Sanisha had genuinely lost count of the number of years.

'Six years, four months, twenty days, sixteen hours and fifty seconds later,' Ashvamedha said nonchalantly.

'You and your precision! What are you doing here?' Had it been some other friend, Sanisha would have hugged him, but not Ashvamedha. She respected him a bit too much and yet desired him, but not physically. It was complicated.

'I teach here,' he said.

'Whoa! Teaching and all? When did that happen? I thought you must be in some big corporate job, earning a lot of money.'

'It's a far more peaceful job.'

'I agree.' Sanisha wasn't surprised. If anyone among them had the balls to kick a lucrative career away and settle for something that was meaningful, it had to be him.

'What about you?' he asked.

'I'm here for a friend. Her kid studies here. Professionally, I too left the corporate world a couple of years ago. I'm working with an NGO. I stay with Adhik. How is Sama?' Sanisha asked. She had always been jealous of his girlfriend,

Sama Akhtar. She yearned for someone like Ashvamedha too. But mostly, she was happy with Adhik.

'She is good. We have been married for some years now,' he said.

'That's awesome!' Something burnt inside her, but she kept smiling.

There was an awkward pause. She heard her name being called. Shweta was standing by a cab.

'I think I'll have to leave. But you know what? We should meet up someday for dinner. All four of us. What say?'

'Yes, why not.'

'Great. Give me your phone number,' Sanisha asked, ready to punch his number into her phone.

'I don't have a mobile phone. You give me your number. I will call you.'

No mobile phone? That's weird, Sanisha thought but gave him her number anyway. Ashvamedha closed his eyes while listening to her. She knew he would never forget the digits. He had the sharpest mind she had ever come across. And the bravest of hearts.

'Do call, else the next time we meet I won't spare you,' Sanisha said.

'Sure.' Ashvamedha smiled.

Sanisha got into the cab. Although Shweta kept talking about her son, Sanisha's mind was elsewhere.

In the next one hour, she reached home. Adhik opened the door. One look at him and she knew what he was up to. She had asked him repeatedly if she had to make dinner but he had insisted that she shouldn't. And now looking at the mess on his apron, she knew that nothing had been made.

'Why do you have to try when you can't improve?' she asked, walking straight into the kitchen. It was messier than his apron.

'I'm sorry. I really thought I would be able to prepare the white sauce pasta myself.'

'Who is going to clean this mess now?' Sanisha placed her hands on her waist.

'I will, I swear. But don't get angry, please,' Adhik said.

'Give me one reason why I shouldn't after seeing this.'

'That's because you look sexy when you get angry. And then I get an erection.'

'Shut up, Adhik!'

Adhik looked down at his groin. He had a boner.

'You men!' Sanisha went out of the kitchen. He followed her into the bedroom. As she took off her top, he started kissing her torso.

'Adhik, move. I'm sweaty.'

'That's lovely,' Adhik said, sniffing her.

'Fuck you, pervert!' Sanisha said, trying to push him away but in vain. He pushed her against the wall and, pinning her hands behind her head, started smooching her. After kissing for half a minute, Sanisha got a little wet. He unbuttoned her jeans, she pushed his boxer shorts down. He wasn't wearing any underwear. Sanisha managed to take off his T-shirt as well, while he helped her get rid of the bra. They collapsed on the bed with Adhik on top. It took him no time to get inside her.

'Fuck, you are too wet!'

'Are you going to make use of it or not?' she asked.

Adhik smirked at her and started thrusting. At that moment, Sanisha wondered how many times they had had normal sex. It was always anger-sex or hate-sex or break-up-sex or make-up-sex. They changed positions. She rode him hard making him come within minutes. She collapsed on his chest. After lying motionless for some time, they cleaned up the mess in the kitchen together and ordered a pizza for Adhik.

'You know I met Ashvamedha today,' Sanisha said as Adhik gobbled up one slice of his pizza after another. Although he was a vegetarian Brahmin, he didn't shy away from having meat outside Agra, his home town.

'Ashvamedha?'

'Don't tell me the name doesn't ring a bell.'

'Oh, Ashva! Where did you meet him?'

'I'd picked Shweta and her son from the school today. Met him there. He teaches at that school.'

'Ashva is a schoolteacher?'

'Why? Where did you see him last?'

'I had last seen him when Parth, Satyam and I were working on a project of an oil company together. But he being a schoolteacher now is a little . . .'

'I know what you mean. Even I was a little surprised. He was a fucking scholar! The best in our batch. Perhaps the best in all the batches ever,' Sanisha remarked.

'He was thrown out, if you remember?' There was spite in Adhik's voice, which Sanisha thought was uncalled for.

She always had an inkling that Adhik had never liked Ashvamedha. Or maybe he didn't like the fact that she liked him too much.

'For taking a stand. I simply can't forget that day. He slapped the chancellor, man! That too in front of the entire institute. He knew his career could get over and still he did it.'

'I thought that was really stupid of him.' Adhik had finished his pizza. He wiped his mouth with a tissue and drank some Diet Coke.

'Stupid? Really? Ashva did what no other man could do.' Sanisha took the can from him and finished it. 'He took a stand for a girl. The chancellor had sexually harassed her. We all knew about it. But none of us had the balls to say it. Neither you nor I.'

'That's all the more reason why I'd say it was stupid. Why would you risk your career for someone you don't know? It would have been okay had she been his girlfriend.' Adhik stood up and went to the bedroom.

Sanisha realized that he wouldn't understand her. She joined him in the bedroom.

'What about that Muslim girlfriend of his? She was hot,' Adhik asked.

Sanisha gave him a you-are-impossible look and said, 'Sama Akhtar. They are happily married now.'

'Good for him.'

'Lucky girl,' Sanisha sighed.

'Is it what I sense it is?'

'What do you sense, Adhik?' Sanisha was lying on the bed beside him.

'All right, confession time. Your eyes always light up when you talk about him. Tonight is no different. Have you ever had feelings for Ashva? You can be honest. I won't mind.'

'You know, he made me realize that courage is the ultimate sex appeal. His masculinity isn't about growing big and beefed-up with protein shakes. There is an inherent magnetism in him. His eyes . . . they exude the unflinching strength in his soul. His poise tells me he holds a storm within and can unleash it whenever he wants to. No gym can help a man get that. You know that this man hasn't ever taken anything lying down. Ashvamedha can destroy everything around him but knows how to control his urges and be humane. That's an intoxicating trait in a man, trust me. That level of self-control in today's reckless times . . . fuck, it melts me.'

'Wow! I asked you a simple question and you gave me a bloody thesis.'

'I respect him. And when a woman respects a man, she can't help but have the kind of glimmer in her eyes that you mentioned.'

'Okay. I asked. You answered. End of the Ashvamedha story.'

There was silence. Then she felt Adhik turning towards her.

'Mumma called in the evening.'

'That she does every evening, so?'

'She said they received a marriage proposal last week.'

'Whose marriage?' Sanisha sat up.

'Mine, of course.'

'And what did you say?'

'The obvious. I asked her to show me the girl's pictures. Her name is Priyanshi Mishra.'

'You are gone, asshole!' Sanisha said and pounced on him like a lioness.

'*Arrey*, don't worry, I've been told she has an elder brother as well. We could have a kinky foursome.'

'Fuck you, pervert!' She pulled his hair as hard as she could. A wrestle ensued, Sanisha scratching and beating Adhik. He held her hands and, in no time, tamed her with his strength. They looked deeply into each other's eyes, gasping for air. Both knew another anger-sex session was due before they called it a night.

27

Adhik had left for office a long time ago. Sanisha had flexible working hours and planned to go to office after lunch. Her maid asked for the clothes. Sanisha had set aside an entire suitcase full of old clothes to give her. While checking it for the last time, she found a dress that used to be her favourite at one point of time. It was a normal-looking salwar-kameez, one of her first in New Delhi. She smiled, thinking about the girl she used to be back then. From someone who didn't know what to do when a stranger gaped at her to someone who no longer thought twice before knocking out such a person, she had really changed. And much of it was because of Adhik.

It was love at first sight for Adhik, or so he claimed. Sanisha was too scared to even think about any romantic prospects back then. She was shy, scared and was always worried about what her family would think if they found out that she had a boyfriend. Adhik, on the other hand, asked her out eighty-eight times in the two years of their master's. And she rejected him that many times. She thought he would forget about her once they completed their post-graduation. But she was surprised to see him in the same MBA institute.

He said it was a coincidence, but she knew otherwise. It was only then that Sanisha, coaxed by her batchmates into believing that a boy who could pursue her for so long in spite of being rejected so many times had to love her genuinely, finally said yes the ninety-third time he asked her out.

Adhik introduced her to many things—alcohol, weed, porn, sex, adventure sports, rave parties, driving without a licence, getting drunk near India Gate at night, and not giving a fuck about what society thought about her and Adhik. He had unlocked a Sanisha in her that she never knew existed.

Although Adhik swore by his love, he hadn't told his parents about her and neither had she. Sanisha was waiting for him to do it first. She knew she could fight with her entire family if only Adhik's family accepted her.

'I'll need some time, baby,' he always said the same thing. And time she gave him. It had been six years since they started dating and three years since they began living together, but that time hadn't come yet. While Adhik's parents were hyper conservative, Sanisha's were selectively liberal due to pressure from their extended family.

'But what's marriage, really? Society's licence to fuck and reproduce?' Adhik would say whenever this topic cropped up.

'Maybe. But you and I can't challenge an institution whose result we both are. Just imagine, if tomorrow we want to plan a family, would you be able to explain to our child why he or she was planned out of wedlock? It's okay to be liberal as long as you're not ostracized by society.' Sanisha's argument stemmed from a deep-rooted frustration that she had as she knew time had already run out. They were on extra time. At least she was. Sooner or later, her father would call her and tell her that someone he knew, probably a friend's son, was waiting to take his family legacy forward through her womb. She knew her father's circle well. They didn't require a woman as a daughter-in-law. All they needed was a baby-making machine.

'All right. The day we decide to have a baby, we will get married, I promise,' Adhik had said. Sanisha knew that wasn't a solution but she kept mum. And now, while looking at the maid sorting her old clothes, she wondered about what Adhik had told her about a proposal last night. Why didn't he get it? It was high time they told their parents about each other and got hitched. Parents' consent wasn't something Sanisha was worried about. Having lived together for so many years, they were already in a domestic set-up. Adhik had become as much a part of her life as she was of his. She simply couldn't think of life without him. All she wanted was their parents to know. Consent for a marriage and knowledge of a relationship are two different things. Sanisha wanted the latter. This much she owed to her parents for all their support.

The maid left with almost all her old clothes. Sanisha not only cooked her lunch, but also packed Adhik's as well. They could afford a cook but Adhik was a fan of her cooking. She liked cooking for him too. On the days she went to office after lunch, she would drop Adhik's lunch off at his office.

Adhik was already salivating. Sanisha had made his favourite dish, chole. While Adhik was relishing it in his office canteen with his colleagues, his mother called to say she was sending him Priyanshi Mishra's picture and that she had shared his number with her. Adhik became a little cross. He thought it was rude to share his number without asking him first. But when was he able to say anything to his mother? He cut the call, annoyed. Seconds later, a picture popped up on his phone. He knew his younger sister must have helped her technologically challenged mother to send the picture via WhatsApp. All his irritation vanished the moment he saw the picture. Priyanshi Mishra's eyes, nose, lips and face . . . Adhik couldn't take his eyes off her.

Bhaiya, this is Priyanshi. She has impressed Mummy and Papa. She will call you soon. Call Mummy after you have had a talk with her. It was Adhik's sister texting him from her mother's phone.

Okay, he responded.

There are certain insects that only need a tiny hole to get inside a house and turn it upside down. Priyanshi Mishra was that insect. And Adhik's decision to talk to her was that tiny hole.

28

It was when Adhik had left for home in his car that he got the call. He answered it through the car's Bluetooth.

'Am I talking to Adhik Sharma?' It was the sweetest voice he had ever heard.

'Yes, who is this?' Adhik asked even though he had guessed who the caller was.

'Hi, this is Priyanshi Mishra. Your mother gave me your number. She asked me to have a chat with you.'

She already sounded like an obedient daughter-in-law, Adhik thought, and said, 'Hi, Priyanshi, how are you?'

For the first time in Adhik's life, a girl had approached him. He wasn't that handsome boy who made girls go weak in their knees. He was okay-looking, of average height and not much charm. When he and Sanisha had started dating, his college friends had said that she was the only highlight in his life as far as girls were concerned. It wasn't just about Adhik's looks. Unfortunately, he just wasn't distinctive in any way. And so, when a beautiful girl like Priyanshi had herself called him up, that too with a marriage proposal, he couldn't help but feel excited.

Only he knew how much he had had to run after Sanisha before she agreed to go out with him. It was like a dream come true. Sanisha Singh was popular among the boys in the MBA institute. The only advantage Adhik had was that he could easily make friends with anyone. If you spent half an hour with him, you'd end up feeling that you'd known him for half a decade. He used the bro-code to his advantage, ensuring that everyone knew that Sanisha was *his* girl. His only threat was Ashvamedha Chauhaan. He knew Sanisha liked him. But as Adhik's luck would have it, Ashvamedha was not only an oddball, according to him, but also had a steady girlfriend, Sama Akhtar. So he had nothing to worry about. And ever since Sanisha had said yes to him, their relationship had gone smoothly, without any major bumps. The only thing he had never told Sanisha was that he had told his parents about her. He had even showed them her picture but they refused to accept a non-Brahmin working woman into their family. And although he knew that Sanisha loved him to death, he also knew that she would never compromise her career for anybody. It was her identity and according to her, identities were a non-negotiable part of someone's life. Apart from being a working woman, she could also become a wife but she wouldn't let the latter eclipse the former.

Adhik knew that his parents wouldn't compromise. From that day onwards, he started pretending to be a liberal. He knew that the shelf life of his relationship wasn't very long, but for that limited time he wanted to possess Sanisha in the name of love and for as long as he could.

He was the one who proposed living together even though he didn't believe in such a set-up. He secretly believed in getting married. But he also knew that if he told the truth to Sanisha, they would break up and she would probably get married to someone else. Adhik neither had the balls to stand up against his parents nor was he willing to be honest with her and let her go. She was a strong-willed woman. And this was what Adhik loved the most about her, but this was also what he feared the most. She was a woman who valued her self-esteem more than anything. She was a woman who could sacrifice but would never compromise in love. They were living together not because he had convinced her to do so, but because somewhere down the line she too had wanted it. A woman like Sanisha could never be tamed or manipulated.

'I'm good. How are you?' Priyanshi asked.

Adhik increased the volume of the speaker and said, 'I'm good.' There was an awkward pause. Neither spoke. It becomes difficult to carry on a conversation with a prospective match about whom you don't know anything.

'So . . .' he said.

'Nothing much. I hope you know why I'm calling you,' she said.

'All I know is that my mother liked your profile on some matrimonial site, thanks to my sister. And she wanted us to talk.' Adhik wanted to lighten the mood before it became more awkward.

'My bhaiya liked your profile too.'

'Where does your brother stay?'

'He works in Mumbai. And I'm in Delhi.'

'Oh, cool. Even I'm in Delhi.'

'I know.'

'Of course!' Adhik said, guessing she must have been told everything about him. Everything his mother knew about him, that is.

'Are you from Delhi?' he asked.

'No, I'm doing a course here in interior designing.'

'I should have guessed. It had to be some course. My mother has a thing against working women.'

'I understood. I told her I would be designing only my house after our marriage.'

Adhik frowned. *Our marriage*. It made him nervous for a second.

'After my marriage, I meant,' she corrected herself. They talked for a few more minutes before saying goodbye. When Adhik reached home, he sat in his car in the parking and looked her up on Facebook, but couldn't find her. Then he tried Instagram. And there she was. 'Priyanshi Mishra'. It was a private account. But he noticed that she was already following him as he had a 'follow back' option. Maybe he had missed the notification. Since she was already following him, he thought it was all right to follow her back. He tapped on it. Her profile opened up. There were around 200 pictures. And he couldn't help but wonder at how gorgeous she was. He went back and saved the number she had called him from. He was about to get out of his car when he received a WhatsApp message from Priyanshi.

Sorry, I didn't know how to say it straight. Actually, bhaiya thinks it's always good to meet up once. If that's okay with you.

Adhik smiled. This too was happening for the first time. A girl wanted to meet up, that too such a gorgeous one.

Sure, we can meet up, he responded. *Meeting someone never caused any damage*, Adhik thought, locked his car and went towards the elevator. What he didn't know was that Priyanshi Mishra had been Erina for Kashvi and Ananya for Dhrithi.

29

Adhik edited out the entire incident of talking to Priyanshi when Sanisha asked him how his day had gone. A simple, everyday question but Adhik's response turned it into a bend in their relationship. And how often do we recognize these bends when they occur? More often than not, the dead end is what hits us. And a futile analysis of what-went-wrong, where-it-went-wrong and how-it-went-wrong is made. Every relationship is governed by certain unsaid rules. And unlike what people popularly think, the first cardinal rule of any relationship isn't loyalty. It's honesty.

It was Sanisha's routine to call her mother every night after dinner. Sometimes her father talked to her as well. And for the last few months the one word that had kept cropping up in these conversations was marriage. Sanisha was always tempted to tell her mother about Adhik, that they were living in and had figured out that they would go on to live a life together. But she stopped herself. She knew that once her mother knew about it, then her father would know it too. And Sanisha wanted to tread carefully. She knew she would convince them only if Adhik gave her a go-ahead from his parents.

'Any idea when you will talk to your parents?' Sanisha asked as they shared a smoke standing on the balcony of their high-rise apartment.

'About?' Adhik asked, blowing out smoke and looking at her.

'About our marriage, of course!' Sanisha took a long drag.

'You know I don't believe in it,' he said, watching her blow out the smoke a tad quicker.

'We've had that discussion already. You may not believe in it, but my family does and so does yours. Do you really think they are going to allow us to stay like this forever? Won't they ever get to know that we stay together?'

'I know we will have to tell them one day.'

'And I'm asking you when that day is going to come. My mother has been passive-aggressively mentioning it to me time and again. I know sooner rather than later that my time's going to be up. Do you want me to marry someone else?' She stubbed the cigarette in the ashtray. She expected a quick response, but Adhik took a while to answer.

'Of course not. I would never want you to marry anyone else. And you know it.'

'Then, Adhik,' she came close and hugged him gently, 'Please talk to your parents. I don't like pressuring you. I've full faith in you. In us. We have given so much time to each other, to this relationship. I can't afford to give it away because our parents don't like it.' She broke the hug, looked into his eyes and added, 'You understand me?'

Adhik nodded.

Three days later, Adhik met Priyanshi over lunch at a restaurant close to his office. His first thought was that her pictures didn't do justice to her beauty. She hadn't even put on a lot of make-up and yet looked so beautiful. It was after they had ordered their food, vegetarian, because he didn't want her to know the truth, that Priyanshi took out a box from her bag and placed it on the table.

'What's this?'

'I've made something for you. Your mother told me you are a foodie,' Priyanshi said. He noticed that she never looked at him directly. Even if she did, it was for less than a second. It made him more interested in her. He took the box and opened it to find Badam Paneer, his favourite. It was something his mother always made at home.

'How did you . . . ?' He left his sentence unfinished after guessing the obvious. The smile on Priyanshi's face told him she understood him as well. 'Your mother told me.'

'I realized,' Adhik said, smiling. It was as good as his mother's. But he didn't tell her about it.

'So, where are your parents? Agra?'

'My parents are no more. My bhaiya is everything to me. He will be happy we met. He says it's important to meet a person regarding these matters.'

They kept chatting, time flew and before he knew it, they had been talking for two hours. It was only when his colleague called him that Adhik realized that he had to rush back to office. When he sat on his bike, Priyanshi asked, 'I don't know if I should say this but are we meeting again?'

Adhik wore his helmet and said, 'Sure we are,' and drove off. He wondered what had made him tell her they would meet again. And he knew the answer as well. Priyanshi brought with herself the promise of a comfortable life because she had already been accepted by his parents. After meeting her he knew she would make a great housewife. The kind the average Indian man not only wished for, but was also subliminally trained for since childhood. But this was in stark opposition to what Sanisha and he were heading towards. Sanisha's words that sooner or later he would have to tell his parents resounded in his mind. Only he wasn't sure what exactly he would tell them.

30

Sanisha was working from home that day. While her colleagues had gone for some excursion in the outskirts of Delhi, she had chosen to skip it. After working till afternoon, she received a call from Shweta. She too hadn't gone for the excursion.

'Up for coffee? I'm here to pick up my son from school. I can meet you at Ambience,' Shweta said. The word school immediately brought someone back to Sanisha's mind. She was up for coffee. But only with him.

'I'm not feeling that well. Just wanted to rest.'

'Oh, never mind. You take care. Hope it is nothing serious. Do you want me to drop by?'

'No, no . . . you carry on. We'll have coffee some other day.'

After the call, she got ready and took a cab to the school. There was a sea of kids around her. She waited till she saw the man she wanted to meet. She walked up to him.

'I'm sorry if it seems weird but you didn't call me, and I wanted to talk to you,' Sanisha said. Her job made her meet all sorts of people. And that, over the years, had turned her bolder than she used to be in college.

'I didn't get the time,' Ashvamedha said. He seemed happy seeing her again.

'I can understand. But now you will have to give me half an hour. Coffee?'

'I prefer chai.'

'Even better. Haven't had the tapri chai from some time now.'

'Let's go. There's one right beside the school,' Ashvamedha said.

They started walking side by side towards the tapri. She still felt the same way about him, something that had never happened with any other man. Not even Adhik.

'How is Sama? Is she working or . . .?' she asked.

'She is working with a bank. It's important to work. Keeps one's self-worth intact.'

'I so agree. But what about people who think working women can never make homes?' she asked. He glanced at her. They had reached the tapri. Once they were holding the cups in their hands, Sanisha clarified, 'I won't lie. I came to meet you out of my own interest. So, don't mind, please.'

'Why would I mind? Our own interest without which we would all be islands unto ourselves, that's what makes us so social these days. At least you are being honest about it.'

'How did you convince your parents about Sama? Or she convince hers?' Sanisha was to the point. She not only wanted to meet Ashvamedha, but also wanted an answer to the question plaguing her and to which Adhik, clearly, had no answer.

'People are convinced not by what you explain to them, but by your conviction in the explanation,' he said.

As the words slowly seeped in, making sense, Sanisha realized that everything she had imagined about Ashvamedha was true.

'I told her parents I might belong to a different religion, but if there was one man who would respect their daughter and her choices forever, then it was me.'

'You never told them that you loved her?'

'No. I wanted them to *see* that I loved her.' There was no obvious emotion on his face when he said it.

And say it, of course, Sanisha thought. 'You know there's so much I want to discuss about Adhik and myself. I don't know where to start.'

She watched him finish his tea.

'We should meet for a longer time then. Right now, Sama must be back from office. And I have the responsibility of preparing the evening tea for us,' he said with a smile.

Sanisha prayed for the Ashva–Sama love story to always remain insulated from life's storms. She'd read about perfect love stories in books, but she had the feeling she was witnessing one in real life that day.

'Sure. When do we meet next?' she asked.

'I work half-days on Saturdays. So, if you can come here then we can sit and talk over coffee.'

'But you prefer chai, right?'

'You gave in to my preference today. It will be my turn the next day. That's how friendships last,' he said.

'Sure,' Sanisha said, smiling.

'But before we leave, I have a question for you.'

'What?'

'What's happiness for you, Sanisha?' Ashvamedha asked.

Sanisha thought for a while and answered pensively, 'I don't think I have a definition for it.'

Ashvamedha smiled and said, 'Okay.' And in his mind, he thought, *you will soon have one.* They both took different cabs to their different destinations.

Adhik came home earlier than usual. Just before lunch, he had received a call from Priyanshi saying that she would come to meet a friend whose office was close to his. If he was free, then they could have lunch together. Adhik found himself saying why not. He joined her, they ate together talking about nothing important. The more he got to know her, the more he felt scared. Priyanshi was a woman he wouldn't have to fight with his parents to get married to; he wouldn't even have to hide any aspect of his life from them. His mother had called him up after Priyanshi had told her that they had met for lunch the other day.

'What do you think, beta? Isn't she the perfect one?' his mother had asked.

He knew she was right, but said, 'I need some time, Ma. We don't know each other at all.'

'What do you need some time for? This isn't some love thing of yours. If you need time, then you'll have to do the roka. After that you can wait for another of six months to know whatever it is that you need to know.' It sounded like an ultimatum. The kind he had been listening to since he was a kid. When he wanted to play cricket, he was given an ultimatum to forget the game and focus on his studies. When wanted to pursue sociology, he was given an ultimatum to study engineering. He wanted to opt out of campus placement and start a business, but was given an ultimatum and had to do an MBA and later, sign up for a high-flying corporate job. He had never challenged his parents. But somewhere down the line, he had turned into an escapist. The only thing he had done without his parents' knowledge was to date Sanisha.

'I'll tell you soon,' he told his mother on the phone. He could hear her happiness as she relayed it to his father and sister. The fact that he hadn't rejected Priyanshi was a confirmation in itself. After the lunch, Adhik felt he would be better off at home. He had fallen asleep when Sanisha came back.

'You came back early?' she asked, heading to the kitchen to prepare some coffee.

'Yeah. Where were you?' he stood outside the kitchen, yawning.

'I had gone to meet Ashvamedha,' she said.

Adhik frowned. 'Where?'

'His school. He teaches there.'

'Why?' He knew there was a tinge of jealousy in his tone. He felt betrayed. Sanisha turned to give him a look. She wasn't used to a 'why' from him.

'What "why"? He is a friend, that's why!'

'I don't like it,' he said and went away. Sanisha patiently waited till the coffee was ready. Then she took the mugs and found him sitting in the balcony. He was sulking.

'You don't like *him*. When will you learn to come to the point directly?' she said casually and offered a mug to him.

'When you already know what it's about, then why do I have to say it out loud?' he said, flinging his arms. His hand hit Sanisha's and one of the mugs fell on the ground, breaking into pieces while coffee spilled all over the balcony.

'I wanted to discuss us with him.' Sanisha was enraged.

'Us? What about us?' Adhik got up, careful not to step on any broken piece, and stood by the balcony door.

'What about us do you think?' she asked, sipping the coffee while holding her mug with both hands. She sat down on the sofa, crossing her legs. She seemed pissed.

'How would he have a solution to anything that concerns us?'

'He is smarter and has way higher EQ and IQ than both of us put together.'

'When I've told you, I need some time to tell my parents about you, then what's this going to weird people and discussing our private stuff?' Adhik guessed what Sanisha had in mind.

'You've been telling me this since we decided to live together. I don't know if you understand this or not, but time is running out for me. My parents want me to get married. And it's not the first time I'm telling you this. Although I do hope it's the last.'

'My parents also want me to get married,' he shot back. There was a helplessness in his response, which Sanisha couldn't decode clearly.

'Then what's the problem? Even we want it!' She sounded slightly choked. Adhik could see her eyes were moist. He only wished he could tell her what it was that was stopping him from answering her. It wasn't even a problem. For problems have solutions. This one was a roadblock. The kind that made you take a different route.

It was while Adhik was sitting alone in the balcony and smoking all the remaining cigarettes in his pack that night, that he figured out how he would answer her question. He knew she wouldn't agree but he would use his favourite way of going about it. Edit and tell.

31

In the week that followed, Adhik intentionally picked up fights with Sanisha over petty issues. She got alarmed as he wasn't short-tempered, but failed to understand that these were underhanded tactics to make her feel that they were not meant to be together. He wanted to push her into believing that their relationship wasn't working out any more. The fights kept intensifying but Sanisha never showed any sign of reaching a saturation point. Finally, weeks later, he dropped the final bomb on her. He was sure this would take care of what hadn't happened in the last few weeks.

'My parents are visiting,' Adhik told her flatly. He was finishing his breakfast. Sanisha was in the kitchen, preparing lunch. She smiled and came into the dining room.

'Finally you told them. I'm so damn happy!' She gave him a peck on the cheek.

'They don't know yet. They just wanted to come here because they were missing me. I couldn't convince them against it.' He again told her a half-truth confidently. His parents were visiting him to finalize his marriage.

Sanisha rolled her eyes, saying, 'When will you convince them about anything, Adhik? I don't know what it is that doesn't make you tell them about us?' She was irritated. She kicked the kitchen door before entering it. Adhik smirked. He was glad his ploy was working. He had thought a lot about it and, in the end, reached a decision: between Sanisha and his parents, he would have to bow down to his parents. He wasn't ready to fight for Sanisha with his parents. He had known one day he would have to face such a situation. He always knew his parents wouldn't accept Sanisha; he also knew that he would have to accept his parents' decision, but he had assumed that Sanisha would make sacrifices for him to become the daughter-in-law that his parents wanted. Now he knew that was a far cry. Sanisha would never stop working. And what about her independent mind? He wouldn't be able to alter it. He loved Sanisha, but knew they couldn't get married to each other. But he didn't have the courage to tell her this directly. She might go to Agra and tell his parents what he had been up to all these years with her. The complication that would ensue was something he didn't even want to think about. His plan was to simply prove to Sanisha that they, as a couple, weren't who they used to be six years ago.

'And what will you do when they come here and see me? Who will you introduce me as?' Sanisha hollered from the kitchen.

Adhik took his plate and went to the kitchen. He kept it in the sink and said, 'You'll have to stay at a friend's place for three days. I will talk to them about us. But I don't want them to discover that we have been living together before I tell them about us.' Another half-truth.

Sanisha took a moment to swallow her anger. But if this would make him talk to his parents about them, she was willing to move out. She promised herself that she would call up Shweta that day itself.

'When are they coming?' she asked.

'Day after,' Adhik said. He was about to leave when he heard her say, 'Will you give me a hug?'

Adhik nodded and hugged her. But Sanisha felt that the hug was awkward.

In the evening, Adhik met Priyanshi. She said she couldn't select a dress for herself and was wondering if he would help her. He was there at the Saket mall in the next one hour. He was amazed to see how much his choices matched hers. And the fact that she always asked him before trying on any dress massaged his ego. Sanisha had never sought his opinion on her clothes. She wore what she wanted. The more he spent time with Priyanshi, the more Adhik grew confident that he was doing the right thing. He had to marry a girl who would listen to him and not someone who had a mind of her own. The more they talked, the more he liked the fact that Priyanshi always agreed with whatever he said. Not like Sanisha, who always countered his opinion. Sanisha was worth the chase in college but it was Priyanshi who easily fitted into his idea of a 'perfect' domestic partner.

'You should have happened to me before,' he said, when they sat down for coffee after Priyanshi had finally bought a dress.

'Before what or whom?' she asked.

Adhik looked at her for a moment. He had still not told her about Sanisha. He would not. Adhik nodded and said, 'Just before now.'

Three days later, Sanisha shifted with her belongings to Shweta's place a day before Adhik's parents were supposed to arrive. She'd cleaned the flat such that his parents would never doubt that he was staying there with anyone else. She only had one thing to tell Adhik before she left the place.

'Please don't disappoint me this time. Tell them, explain it to them and convince them. I'm sure they will understand.'

'Yeah, I will,' Adhik nodded. He had made up his mind. He would agree to marry Priyanshi if his mother insisted. Later, he would tell Sanisha that he was pressured into taking such a decision. What could she do? He wasn't committing a crime. She might cry, but eventually she would have to move on.

In the evening, a visitor arrived at Shweta's flat. Sanisha was surprised to find it was Ashvamedha.

'That's my son's tuition teacher,' Shweta introduced him. Sanisha told her they were friends and had met the other day at school. They exchanged greetings but talked only once he was done teaching Shweta's son and another neighbour's child together. Shweta had gone to the market and the children were playing in the next room. Sanisha prepared some tea.

'Do you live here?' Ashvamedha asked.

'No. I live with Adhik but his parents are coming tomorrow so I . . . he hasn't told them about us yet,' she said. For some reason, she felt she could talk to him without hiding anything. She waited for a reaction. None came.

'But this time he is going to talk,' she said.

'And what if he doesn't?' Ashvamedha said it so casually that for a moment Sanisha thought she had misheard him. She took her time to answer.

'I don't know. I'll be honest with you. I've a feeling he never will. And we will have to choose different paths soon.'

Ashvamedha could sense her emotions were getting the better of her.

'You know I'm ready to fight the world for him, all I'm seeking is a little confidence from him. He seems to have given up even before the battle has begun. I've tried my best to make him feel that I'll always be there with him even if his parents refuse. Together, we will convince them but . . .' She thought for a moment and then asked, 'Is it possible for a boy who chased a girl for two long years to give up on their relationship of six years without a fight?' Her voice choked when the last words came out. Ashvamedha remained quiet. He understood Sanisha was introspecting. She didn't really need an answer. She probably knew it already.

'Life can be such a bitch, I tell you,' she said, holding her face in her hands.

'Don't judge life based on where you are at this moment. Judge when that moment is a thing of the past. You'll see how every bad moment was actually designed for some good reason.'

She looked at him. His eyes were on her.

'You'll be safe, Sanisha,' he said. The assurance sounded cryptic. Safe from what? Adhik? Or did he mean the emotional chaos that would unleash if they broke up?

While Sanisha was hoping against hope that Adhik would talk to his parents about them, sweets were being distributed back home. Priyanshi was there, so were Adhik, his parents and his sister. Their match was made. His parents told Priyanshi they would talk to her elder brother and fix a date for the roka. When it was time for Priyanshi to leave, Adhik decided to drop her to her place. He dropped her home and then left.

As Priyanshi opened the door of her flat, she was pulled inside by her supposed elder brother, Kunal Mishra.

'Did the fucker touch you?' he asked. There was rage in his eyes.

'Of course, not,' she said. 'You think I'm going to let him touch me?'

Kunal relaxed. Priyanshi had an amused smile on her face.

'I'm glad though. Now you know how I felt when you were fucking Dhrithi.'

'Shut up! My mind, heart and soul—nothing was in it.'

'Yeah, yeah, I know,' she said, closing the door behind her, and added, 'You had dinner?'

'Yeah, but I'm here to show you something,' he said and took out an envelope from his pocket. He gave it to her. She took out the two slips of papers that it contained. Looking at them, her eyes immediately turned moist. She hugged him.

'Is it really happening?' she asked, looking at the two tickets to Amsterdam.

'It is. Just a matter of time now.'

'I can't wait any more.'

'We'll have to. This is the last phase. We have been smart till now. Just a little more work left.'

Priyanshi nodded.

'Now WhatsApp me the photographs you clicked at Adhik's place.'

She quickly sent him the photographs.

'And the countdown begins,' he said, looking at the pictures and kissing her hand.

32

The apartment complex where Shweta lived was not very big, but was well-maintained. It had a small park for the children to play and a few benches for the elders to sit and chat. Kunal sat on one of the benches for an hour with his eyes fixed on the entrance. Another fifteen minutes later, he saw Sanisha entering through the main gate. He accosted her before she could take the lift to her building.

'Are you Sanisha Singh?' he asked.

'Yes. Do I know you?' she was surprised.

'I'm Kunal Mishra. We should talk.'

'About?'

'Priyanshi Mishra is my sister.'

Sanisha was lost for a moment. She'd heard the name somewhere. When she finally figured out who it was, she didn't how to react.

'How can I help? And how did you track me?' she asked.

'Don't worry, I'm not stalking you. The Sharma family had got in touch with me through a marriage portal for my sister, who also lives in Delhi. They've met as well.'

'Wait a minute. Are you telling me that Adhik and Priyanshi have met?'

'Yes. Not once but many times. And last night, she was at his place. His parents called me this morning to fix the date for their roka.'

This guy is on dope for sure, this isn't possible, was all that Sanisha could think.

'But Priyanshi is my only sister and family. I couldn't have agreed to the wedding just like that. So, I decided to do a little background check on Adhik. I hired a private detective just to make sure my sister wasn't making a mistake,' Kunal lied.

Sanisha was staring at him wide-eyed.

'And the detective told me he has been living with you for a long time. Is that true?' he asked. He repeated himself when she didn't say anything.

'Do you have any proof of what you just said?' Her mind was stuck on the fact that Adhik had met Priyanshi. Not once but several times.

'I don't have any pictures of them meeting, but these are the photos that were taken last night, which Priyanshi shared with me. She was at Adhik's place along with his parents,' Kunal said and handed his phone to her.

Sanisha kept swiping the photographs till she had checked all of them. In the last two days, she had done a lot of permutations and combinations of all the scenarios that could happen once Adhik's parents were in Delhi. But not once had she considered this possibility. She gave the phone back to Kunal and walked out of the building premises. Kunal sighed and stuffed the phone in his pocket. Half the job was done. The other half was left. He ran behind Sanisha.

'Hello! You didn't tell me if what my detective has said is true,' he said, catching up with her.

Sanisha stopped, looked at him and said, 'I'm going to Adhik's place. If you want, you can come along.'

'I don't want to get into anything personal. The fact that this man lied is enough for me to cancel this alliance,' Kunal said, knowing well that if he met Adhik, the latter would recognize him as Nihit.

'Suit yourself,' Sanisha said and walked off.

When she reached the flat, Adhik was at home. It was his sister who opened the door. Sanisha barged inside. Adhik was shell-shocked to see her.

'Who is she?' Adhik's mother demanded.

'Tell her, Adhik. Who am I? At least now for God's sake tell her who the fuck am I?' Sanisha said. The hurt was pronounced in her voice. And the betrayal was evident in her moist eyes.

'Do you know her?' Adhik's father stood up from the sofa. His mother too stood behind him while his sister came and stood beside Adhik. He stood up shakily.

'I'm Sanisha Singh. And your son has been living with me, claiming that he loves me!' Sanisha said, narrowing her eyes at Adhik.

'Think before you say anything,' Adhik's mother took a step forward. 'We aren't third-class people that you can talk to us like that. We don't know you. You are lying, I'm sure. Isn't it, Adhik?' She turned towards her son. He was quiet.

'Tell her you don't know me. Tell her we haven't lived here for three years. Tell her you never chased me in college.

Tell her you never wanted to tell her about me. Tell her I'm a nobody but you still spent over half a decade with me.' Tears rolled down Sanisha's cheeks.

'I know my son. You must have manipulated him,' Adhik's mother screeched. And she didn't stop.

'I know women like you. First, you will cast a spell on good boys like my son and then blame it on them. And what kind of a woman would live with a man just like that? It just reflects on your upbringing and where you've come from.'

Sanisha took a few steps, passed his mother and stood right in front of Adhik. She said, 'Have you chewed up your tongue? Will you say anything? Was I the one who wanted to move in together? Tell me, Adhik, was I the one who proposed to live together?' She raised her voice.

'Get away from my son! I know it must have been you.' Adhik's mother pushed her away and stood in front of her son. She turned to Adhik and said, 'I know she was the one. Why don't you just say it?'

Adhik looked at his mother and said softly in a victimized tone, 'Yes, Ma, she wanted us to live together.'

Sanisha wanted to kill him. But she couldn't move.

'I knew it. Now you get lost, else we will call the police,' Adhik's mother yelled at her. It took a few seconds for Sanisha to regain the strength to move her legs and leave. There was nothing more left to ask or to answer. She went back to Shweta's place, called up her mother that night and told her she was ready to get married. She asked her to look for a man. She would move back to Bhopal within the next three months. Her mother couldn't believe her ears. Her father came on the line and told her she'd really made him proud and that he would find her the best man possible. Sanisha heard everything but registered little. After the call, she took a couple of sleeping pills, which Shweta took regularly, and went to sleep.

'This was the easiest of the lot, wasn't it?' Priyanshi asked. Of all the names—Erina, Ananya and Priyanshi—she liked Priyanshi the most. She felt it was closest to her real personality.

'Hmm. That's because hers was already a pressure-cooker situation. Sooner or later, this would have happened. I really don't think Adhik would have married her,' Kunal said. They were in a cab on their way back to their flat.

'I agree. But among Kashvi, Dhrithi and Sanisha, I felt really bad for Sanisha. Some men can be such cowards and opportunists that it's unbelievable.'

After some time, Priyanshi said, 'I've learnt a lot about relationships after knowing these women's lives.' She expected Kunal to say something, but he didn't.

'So, what remains of Sanisha and Adhik?' she asked.

'The climax,' Kunal responded.

33

Sanisha woke up in the morning with tears in her eyes. Finding her distraught, Shweta asked what the matter was. She knew Sanisha wasn't the kind of person who cried over petty issues. A little probing, and she opened her heart to Shweta.

'I trusted him. And he . . . he didn't even open his fucking mouth in front of his mother when she was ready to declare me a slut. And when he did, I thought it would've been better if he hadn't.' Sanisha was sobbing uncontrollably. Shweta tried her best to calm her down but in vain. She went to office after asking Sanisha to be at home and rest.

Adhik sent her 143 messages, and seventy missed calls. Sanisha didn't reply to any one of them. After a point, she blocked his number. There was no way she was going to give him another chance. And another chance for what? He had already introduced her to his family as someone who had manipulated him into a relationship. Apologizing over WhatsApp was the easiest. Would he be able to take his mother's words back? Would he be able to salvage her image in front of them? Would he be able to redeem her from the humiliation she suffered due to him and his cowardice last evening?

In the evening, while she was sipping coffee with Shweta in the balcony, the doorbell rang.

'Must be Sonu's teacher,' Shweta said. Sanisha stopped her, saying, 'Do you mind if I talk to him for some time before he teaches Sonu?'

Shweta knew they were friends. She let Sanisha go and open the door. It was Ashvamedha. The way he looked at her eyes, she knew he understood there was something wrong. Shweta said she would prepare some tea for Ashvamedha and excused herself to the kitchen.

'I don't think Adhik and I are getting married,' Sanisha said, without looking at him. She didn't know what exactly she had wanted to talk to him about. Or was it just that she wanted someone to hear her side of the story. Someone who would hear her without judging her or interrupting her in between.

'What do we do when years of emotional investment suddenly seem like a joke one day? How do you fight the frustration when you simply can't go back, undo your biggest mistake that had at one point seemed like a blessing? And what answer do you give yourself when you know you had been right all along. The other person wasn't. In love, why do we have to suffer for others' mistakes? I loved Adhik. I saw a future with him. I lived almost my entire twenties with him. I postponed my parents' plans for me. I was even ready to say goodbye to my parents forever. Can you beat that? Fools like me deserve this, I guess. I should have been practical like Kashvi, who married because she needed someone to pamper her all her life.'

There was silence. Ashvamedha was quietly looking at her. She was looking elsewhere. He understood Sanisha didn't want him to talk. He spoke only when he had taken the first sip of tea, which Shweta had come and left on the centre table before going to her room.

'Did you find the definition of happiness, Sanisha?' he asked.

'Huh?' Sanisha didn't understand his question at first.

'Remember, you had told me you are still trying to find out what happiness is? Have you found out?'

Sanisha took a moment before she replied, 'I don't know what happiness is, but I now know what it is not. It's not something that stays. It is an illusion. A petty, third-grade illusion. Like a cheap roadside magician's silly trick.'

Ah, only she got it right! Ashvamedha thought. 'I think I should teach Sonu now,' he said.

In the evening, Kunal called up Adhik and asked him to meet at the parking lot of a mall. He said he wanted to talk about Priyanshi. Next, he called Sanisha and asked her to meet at the same place, saying he wanted to tell her something important. She was a little reluctant at first, Sanisha eventually agreed after Kunal insisted. While Adhik and Sanisha arrived on time at the parking lot, Kunal didn't. The two were shocked to see each other. Sanisha, realizing it had to be one of Adhik's plans to meet her, dashed towards the exit when Adhik ran after her and held her hand. She wrung it free and pushed him away.

'Don't you dare touch me. You lost all your rights last evening,' she said. She was shivering with anger.

'I know I've been an asshole, but I couldn't go against my parents. They would have never accepted you the way you are. And you wouldn't have ever changed for them.'

'And when were you planning on telling me this? You wanted time, I gave you time. You should have asked for a break-up in the first place. Or was everything a lie?'

'I loved you, Sanisha.'

'Shut up! You never did. If you loved me, you wouldn't have let your mother humiliate me. You only *wanted* me, flaunt me as your girlfriend in college. You always knew we would never make it. Priyanshi was only an excuse. You would have said yes to any girl your mother presented before you who was worth your fancy.'

'Maybe I would have. But that's because you wouldn't have agreed to be a housewife ever. Would you?'

Sanisha looked at him, appalled, and then smirked.

'What?' he asked.

'I'm trying to figure out what I had seen in you for the last several years to believe that we had a future. Now it's all my fault? I'm the one who is responsible for our relationship not working out. Wow! I'm super impressed, Adhik Sharma.' She clapped.

'Listen, Sanisha . . .' Adhik grabbed her hand. She immediately pushed him back with all the force that she could muster.

'Don't you fucking touch me! And don't you fucking "listen Sanisha" me! I think men like you will always have a problem saying these two words, but let me help you out with this. Adhik, "it's over!" Get the fuck out of my life. I will make sure you are out of my memories sooner rather than later. And don't you dare try to meet or reach out to me again,' she said and stormed off.

They didn't know that their fight was being captured on a CCTV camera. While Sanisha went back to Shweta's place in a cab, Adhik headed home to their flat on his bike. On an empty road, when he was speeding, a car appeared from behind. He knew that car. It was Sanisha's. But she never drove it. He slowed down, assuming she wanted to talk to him. But the car, once alongside the bike, took a sudden sharp turn and threw him off. Although Adhik was wearing a helmet, he was grievously hurt. The car, which was indeed Sanisha's, drove away as if nothing had happened. It made sure its number was captured by another CCTV camera installed at the traffic signal where the accident had taken place.

For any third person who watched the two footage, the prime suspect in Adhik's accident or murder would be none other than Sanisha.

BOOK 2

The Best Couple Ever

1

Assistant commissioner of police Abhay Pratap Singh was on his way to UKC's house after three years. The last time he was there, a serial killer was on the loose after killing twenty senior citizens.

Nobody knew what UKC stood for. Maybe his initials?

Abhay asked for a cigarette from his junior, Inspector Vivek Parashar, who was accompanying him to UKC's house. It was his third cigarette in the last one hour.

'Sir, is everything fine?' Vivek asked.

'You have never met UKC, right?' Abhay said, taking a small drag.

'No, sir. But I've heard a lot about him.' Everybody in Delhi Police, from the constables to the commissioner, knew of UKC. He had been a banker till he was thirty-five. Then a near-fatal car accident paralysed him from neck down. After the crash, UKC had developed a peculiar phobia that if his skin was exposed to any form of natural light, it would itch uncontrollably. So he always wore a rain poncho-like garment that also covered his face.

Vivek parked the jeep outside UKC's house in GK 1, and he and Abhay went inside. The house belonged to UKC's father, a former armyman. Now, with no immediate family members alive, he lived alone with his help, Neema. At forty-four, UKC was a bachelor. He received a meagre pension from the bank, and was also paid a monthly stipend by the home ministry for assisting Delhi Police in solving difficult cases.

Neema had been hired right after UKC began his stint with Delhi Police. As she opened the door, Vivek was surprised to see her—a middle-aged woman with a slight stoop and a kind face. She asked them to sit on the bamboo chairs in the living room, while she went inside to get UKC.

'There are two reasons why UKC hired her. One, she prepares amazing chicken soup, and second, she knows three kinds of martial arts. I've seen her pinning down four men in five minutes,' Abhay told Vivek, who was stunned. *Looks can be deceptive*, he thought.

Neema wheeled in UKC. He looked depressed, and had dark circles. He had curly hair and wore thick glasses, which made his eyes look bigger. He glanced at Vivek. The latter found it difficult to digest that this man, who had never gone out of his house in the last several years, had helped solve cases by only using his brains and instincts. The more he looked at UKC, the more Vivek understood that there was a strange aura around the man . . . as if something was totally wrong about him.

'My junior. He will take notes if need be,' Abhay clarified. Vivek sat facing UKC.

'Tea, coffee?' Neema asked the two police officers.

'Tea,' Abhay said. Vivek nodded in agreement. Neema left.

'I can already sniff an interesting case,' UKC said sharply, looking at Abhay.

'You haven't changed at all in the last three years,' Abhay said as he made himself comfortable.

'I have. I was forty-one when we had last met. Now, I'm forty-four. Just because you can't see it, doesn't mean the change isn't there,' UKC said. Taken aback, Vivek looked at Abhay. The latter didn't acknowledge it. Instead, Abhay said, 'Should I start?'

'I would suggest so.'

'All right. So, you must have heard about the Basu family. The ones who run . . .'

' . . . the Basu Multi-Specialty Hospital in Chanakyapuri. The head of the family is trying his hand at politics next year.'

'Exactly! They have lodged an FIR against the daughter-in-law, Kashvi Khandelwal Basu.'

UKC closed his eyes, gesturing Abhay to go on.

'A month ago, Dr Parth Basu was found unconscious and later admitted to the ICU of his own hospital. His wife, Kashvi, had found him in their penthouse. He is brain dead due to a spinal injury. He is breathing with the help of life support. Dr Basu's parents have alleged that his wife was having an affair, which her husband had found out. The couple was having a lot of fights over this issue. His wife even got pregnant allegedly with her lover's child. She has claimed that Dr Basu made her abort it unethically. But there's no proof of it. We have some photographs of the wife with another man.

When we interrogated her, she claimed the man in the photographs was one Nihit Tandon, who had approached her through Instagram . . .'

'What's Instagram?' UKC asked, opening his eyes.

'It's a social media app for uploading photographs,' Abhay explained.

'Man invented technology to make life easier. But has now become so dependent on it that he has turned stupid. I hate technology. I hate smartphones. But above all, I hate men!' UKC declared, closing his eyes again.

Abhay and Vivek exchanged looks before continuing, 'Tandon had allegedly approached the wife because she was a social media influencer.'

UKC opened his eyes but before he could ask Abhay anything, the latter told him what it meant. UKC closed his eyes again.

'Tandon helped her gain mileage as an influencer. He knew Dr Basu as they were both members of the same golf club. Dr Basu's wife has claimed that he had a sister named Erina. And she is sure that Erina and Dr Basu were having an affair. Erina worked at the Basu Multi-Specialty Hospital. We interrogated the hospital staff, but nobody said anything similar.'

Neema came back with two steaming cups of tea. Both Abhay and Vivek gratefully accepted their cups. The tea was so good that Vivek wanted to ask Neema what the secret ingredient was, but he stopped himself. This was not the time for exchanging recipes.

'You interrogated Tandon or his sister?' UKC asked, opening his eyes.

'This is where the case becomes . . . a little absurd,' Abhay said and added, 'we haven't been able to get in touch with either Tandon or his sister so far. Erina Tandon's address in the hospital records is fake. Their phone numbers are not registered under their names. Also, Tandon lied to Dr Basu's wife that he was a pilot with Jet-Set Airlines. Dr Basu's wife has helped us make a sketch of both Tandon and his sister. We have circulated it but no headway has been made till now.'

'Nobody else has seen this Tandon and his sister?' UKC asked.

'The hospital staff have seen the girl. We have CCTV footage of her. And it matches the sketch. But Tandon . . .' Abhay stopped.

UKC looked at him straight.

'He had visited the Basus' penthouse several times, which has a CCTV. But not even a single time was his face captured in the camera. We don't know if this was intentional.'

'So, no one else has seen Tandon?'

'We checked with the swimming club where he and sister were members. No picture or video records. The pool area doesn't have CCTV coverage. Same for the golf club.'

'You said Tandon used to play golf with Dr Basu. Had nobody else seen him during these times?'

Abhay sighed. From what UKC knew of him, he realized the most interesting part of the case was coming up.

'His two close friends did.'

'And they are . . . ?'

'Adhik Sharma and Satyam Vishwanath,' Vivek answered.

'Does their description of Tandon match with that of Dr Basu's wife's?'

'We couldn't get their statements. In fact, we won't be able to,' Abhay said.

'Why not?'

'Because both Adhik Sharma and Satyam Vishwanath are sharing the ICU with Dr Basu. They are both brain-dead as well. They too were attacked around the same time as Dr Basu,' Abhay said.

There was silence for a while. And then UKC laughed out loud.

'Neema, get me the soup. I'm hungry,' he said. His eyes looked even bigger now behind those high-powered specs.

From previous interactions, Abhay knew that UKC demanded chicken soup every time he found a case challenging. And he would not rest till he had cracked it.

'Three close friends . . . all brain-dead. Same modus operandi?' UKC asked.

'No. Dr Basu's spine was intentionally damaged. Sharma had a road accident and is in a coma. And Vishwanath was injected with lead, which produced multiple seizures and eventually brain death.'

'Who are the prime suspects according to you?'

'Dr Basu's wife. Sharma's live-in partner, Sanisha. And so far, we have no suspect in Vishwanath's case.'

'Why is Sharma's partner a suspect?'

'We have CCTV footage of them fighting in the parking lot of a mall minutes before a car hit Sharma's bike. CCTV footage from the intersection where the accident happened revealed that the car belonged to Sharma's partner. But the woman claims it wasn't her. Her alibi has checked out. She was heading home in an Uber cab when the accident happened.'

'Does the partner suspect anyone?'

'No. But Sharma's parents claimed she was unhappy as he was getting married to another girl.'

'Who is this girl?'

'Priyanshi Mishra. Her brother, Kunal Mishra, and only living family member got in touch with his parents through a matrimonial site.'

'Another sister–brother angle?' UKC's eyes darted from left to right before coming to a stop on Abhay.

'Yes, and, interestingly, even they can't be traced. The girl's phone number was registered under a different person's name; her matrimonial site profile can no longer be found and she has deleted her social media accounts. Just like Nihit and Erina Tandon. The same with her brother. We interrogated the people whose names were used for taking the phone connections, but couldn't find anything.'

UKC's eyes were dancing. Abhay knew he was thinking intensely about something. When he spoke, Abhay was baffled.

'Can you smell the chicken soup?' he asked. 'The scent of any food is important. It makes me really hungry.'

If Vivek hadn't already known about UKC, he would have concluded that he was crazy.

'Get me the interrogation videos of the three women: the wives of Dr Basu and Satyam Vishwanath, and Sharma's partner.'

'We haven't interrogated Vishwanath's wife yet. Just routine inquiry. As I mentioned earlier, we haven't zeroed down on a suspect. There is no motive in her case.'

'Don't you remember what I had said? Just because you don't see it, doesn't mean it isn't there,' UKC said and dismissed the session.

2

He had been waiting for this day for some time now. Ashvamedha was standing right in front of the ICU. He could see Adhik lying on a bed, surrounded by medical equipment, pipes attached to various parts of his body. Next to him were Parth and Satyam. He couldn't see them, but he knew they were lying there too, brain-dead. He heaved a sigh of relief. *Work done*, he thought.

Ashvamedha turned to face Sanisha, who was sitting alone on an aluminium seat. He'd told her he got to know about Adhik when he had gone to teach Shweta's son. The school was closed for Diwali. He'd extended his break and was on leave for close to a month. He had joined work only a day ago.

'Where's his family?' Ashvamedha asked. Sanisha gestured towards a man, a woman and a young girl who were sitting a bit far away on another row of seats. The woman was looking at him curiously.

'They still think I've done it,' Sanisha said. The pain in her voice was evident. 'Come, let's go down to the cafeteria,' she said, and stood up. Ashvamedha followed her.

They sat at a corner table. Sanisha looked haggard; the last one month had clearly taken a toll on her.

'What happened?' Ashvamedha asked. Sanisha took less than a minute to tell him everything. Little did she know that it was Ashvamedha himself who had engineered the incidents.

'I wasn't driving that night. I rarely drive my car. It was someone else. I don't know who. Priyanshi and Kunal are suddenly missing. And Adhik's family thinks I'm the culprit. The police have also interrogated me.'

'What about your family?' he asked.

'Mumma and Papa came to Delhi a day after Adhik's accident. They did not know about our live-in arrangement. It was too much for them to digest. There was a major showdown between his parents and mine. I was called names and labeled a witch who spoilt their son's life.' Ashvamedha sensed that she could break down any moment. Half a minute later, she continued, 'They went back to Bhopal the very next day, accusing me of ruining the family's name. I can go back home only if I hand over the reins of my life to them.' Seconds passed; no one said anything. Tears ran down Sanisha's cheeks.

'Believe me, Ashva, I didn't do this to Adhik. Yes, we had a fight. Yes, I thought he was a pig. But I would never kill him! I don't know who was driving my car that night. Just believe me.' She sounded desperate and held his hand. Ashvamedha grasped her hand back, saying, 'I believe you, Sanisha.'

Suddenly, Sanisha felt calm. The world around her was like a hot, dry afternoon, while his touch was a much-needed shade. She walked him out of the hospital a few minutes later.

'May I hug you once?' she asked. A warm, understanding smile appeared on Ashvamedha's face; he nodded. She hugged him and said, 'Thanks. I needed this.'

'I should have told you this before,' Ashvamedha said, 'Don't get so involved with someone that when you have to let them go, you have to do so at the cost of your own sanity.'

Ashvamedha left, leaving behind a pondering Sanisha.

The last one month had been worse than Kashvi's worst nightmare. She had been put under house arrest. To make matters worse, her father-in-law had hired a man to monitor all her movements. She was still reeling from what Nihit had done. He had actually tried to kill Parth. That was not what she had wanted. But before he went missing, he had made her listen to a recording where she heard herself saying: *I won't spare him*. Those words would be enough for Parth's family to press charges and get her locked up forever. She had to be selective about her confession of Nihit. She did tell the police that the man in the photographs was Nihit. But she also stuck to her statement, which was the truth, that she had never had any affair. She understood why Nihit was absconding, but where was Erina? Why didn't she surface after Parth's news came out in the newspapers? Was she scared? That was the only plausible reason Kashvi could think of. Her parents had flown down but Parth's father had threatened them to stay away from her. The only good thing her father-in-law did was to keep the matter as much under the wraps as possible because it could tarnish his political career. Many of Kashvi's Instagram followers knew the media version of what had happened to Parth. It had been a month since Kashvi had posted anything on her social media profiles. She spent every second in fear. What if Nihit surfaced and showed the police the recorded clip? He would be let off scot-free.

But then she was stunned after coming to know that even Satyam and Adhik were brain-dead and admitted to the same hospital. It was one bizarre coincidence. She tried reaching out to Dhrithi but could only meet her and Sanisha in the hospital twice. And today, after a month, when the doorbell rang, she hoped it would be Dhrithi. They had decided to meet at her house.

Kashvi didn't know whether to empathize or feel good about the fact that Dhrithi, like her, looked terrible.

'Where's Sanisha?' Kashvi asked.

'I don't know. Why don't you ping her on WhatsApp? And give me a drink,' Dhrithi said, sinking into the couch. Kashvi made drinks for Dhrithi and herself and joined her on the couch.

'What the fuck happened with Satyam?' Kashvi asked.

'Too much lead consumption,' Dhrithi echoed the medical report. She was secretly glad that the report had not stated how Satyam had consumed lead in such a lethal dose.

That night, when Satyam had come back home, Dhrithi was already rattled by the turn of events. She was sure that the people behind Kshay's death were trying to blackmail her. But why her? Why ask her to choose between herself and her husband? But the stakes were too high. She had to make a decision. And she did. She first mixed sleeping pills, bought over-the-counter, in his beer after dinner. Satyam conked off soon. She readied the syringes. Midway, she hesitated but then realized what would happen if she didn't inject Satyam—everyone would come to know about her affair with Kshay; their one-day Goa visit; and his death. She could be seen very clearly in the video. How would she deny her presence in that room? She cursed herself for everything. Why the fuck did she go to Goa with Kshay! Finally, after making up her mind, Dhrithi injected all the three syringes, one after the other, into Satyam, not knowing what they contained. All that she did know was that if she didn't do it, her life would be ruined forever.

'But lead consumption?' Kashvi sounded suspicious. Dhrithi had told everyone, including the police, that Satyam had come home drunk and gone straight to sleep. She was lucky to escape any suspicion as neither her in-laws nor anyone else had anything against her. What puzzled her was why Ananya had deactivated her Instagram account after Kshay had. She tried to call her a few times, but her phone was always switched off. She concluded that the men behind Kshay's death had got to Ananya as well. She deleted her number before it led to further complications.

As the two women drank together, they discussed their stories, neither telling the other the truth. At the end, they were as perplexed as the police were.

Ashvamedha was putting all the dishes in the kitchen sink. They had just had dinner. He'd updated Sama on Parth, Adhik and Satyam. She asked him what next. To which he'd had no answer. After washing the dishes, he came out of the kitchen and told her, 'You always asked me why I stopped writing poetry. Well, I didn't. I was preparing my magnum opus. And this is it. The police can try their level best. They might get to me. But they will never unravel the inspiration behind this disturbing poem.'

'So, have they arrived at the right definition of happiness like you wanted?' Sama asked.

'The three men can't feel anything, let alone happiness. The two women, I'm sure, now know how wrong their definitions were. Sanisha though somewhat understood it before. By the way, I have to tell you something.'

'What?'

'Sanisha hugged me today at the hospital gate, and I felt something.'

'Like?'

'Like I was betraying you.'

'Come on! I'm sure it was a harmless hug.'

'It was, but it made me uncomfortable, though I didn't tell her anything. I love you, Sama. Not more. Not less. Just the way one should love someone. And I won't spare anyone who comes between you and me. Even if it's my own heart. Or mind. Or feelings.' Ashvamedha was serious.

'One of those things you say,' she said with a heart-warming smile.

'I mean what I say,' he said, and switched off the lights.

3

ACP Abhay and Inspector Vivek were back at UKC's house within a few days. This time, they had brought the videos of the interrogations.

They were waiting in the study this time. Rows of new and old books were neatly arranged on ceiling-high shelves, which lent the room a sombre look. The windows were shut and the curtains drawn. As a result, it was stuffy inside but Abhay knew they weren't in a position to complain. They were glad at least the AC and the lights were on. Neema played the interrogation CDs one at a time. She sat next to UKC with a stopwatch. She knew her job well—she was supposed to clock the reaction time of the person speaking in the video for every question asked and then calculate the average reaction time. UKC had developed a theory based on his experience of interpreting interrogation videos. According to him, anyone who took more than two seconds to respond was more often than not lying. And the ones who took less than 1.5 seconds to respond were either telling the truth or had prepared really well. The catch was to filter out the people who fell under the second category.

The first video was of Kashvi. She was asked basic questions at first—her name, her parents' names, her husband's name, her Gurugram and Kolkata addresses, her school's name, etc. Then she was asked questions whose answers she had to think about—her car's number; what she had worn at her last party. This exercise was done to see how long she would take to recollect something. Finally, she was asked questions related to the case.

Do you know Nihit Tandon? UKC guessed it was Vivek who was interrogating as only Kashvi's face was visible on the screen.

Yes. UKC noted that the answer was instantaneous.

How do you know him?

He approached me via Instagram.

Were you having an affair with him?

No. This too was answered instantaneously, UKC noted.

Do you believe that your husband aborted your child?

Yes.

Why would he do that?

He was having an affair.

With?

Erina, Nihit's sister.

How are you so sure?

I found the same perfume that she wore in our wardrobe. It's impossible to have found it there.

Who else knows about the perfume?

Parth does.

Anyone who can support you in your statement as Dr Basu won't be able to answer?

Kashvi didn't say anything at first and then answered, *nobody else*.

Are you guilty?

I'm innocent. Again instantaneous.

Who do you suspect if you say you are innocent?

Too long a pause before the answer. *I don't know*.

Do you think there is a relation between Dr Basu, Adhik Sharma and Satyam Vishwanath's incidents?

It's improbable!

Do you recognize these persons? She was shown the sketches she had helped the police prepare.

These are Nihit and Erina, Kashvi said. This was her most confident answer.

Thank you, Mrs Basu.

The video ended. UKC glanced at Neema.

'Average time taken to answer the first set of questions is one second. Average time taken to answer the second set of questions is 1.7 seconds. And the average time taken to answer the questions related to the case is 1.3 seconds,' Neema said.

'Thanks, Neema,' UKC said.

'What do you think?' Abhay asked. He noticed UKC's eyes were darting from left to right before coming to a stop on him.

'Mrs Basu's motive could have been to unite with her lover. But the man she was supposedly having an affair with, Tandon, is nowhere to be found.'

'Maybe he plans to surface when we relax a bit about the case,' Vivek chipped in. UKC gave him a look and said, 'Or maybe the person in the photographs isn't Tandon. It is

211

someone else. We only have Mrs Basu's word for it, just like it is only her word for the perfume that she has mentioned.'

There was silence. *Something's not adding up*, UKC thought and said aloud, 'All right. Let's watch the other two.'

Sanisha seemed more forthright with her answers. The last question that was asked of her was:

Do you think Kunal Mishra used your car to kill your boyfriend?

I don't know. All I know is my car was used. But I don't know if it was Kunal. There was no need to kill him.

Adhik Sharma's parents helped us make these sketches. Could you identify these people for us?

That's Priyanshi and that is Kunal.

'Sanisha Singh is right. I don't think Mishra is involved in the accident,' UKC said, after hearing Neema's report. 'Why would a brother want to kill a man who is supposed to marry his sister? Especially when the sister isn't even emotionally invested in him. The argument happened between Adhik and his girlfriend. Mishra had no stake in it. Why would he involve himself, kill a man and make it all the more difficult for himself and his sister? This is absurd. There was someone else in the car. And only when we find out who that person was will we get to know if there is a connection between Dr Basu and Sharma's cases. Of course, the brother–sister angle is uncanny. Especially when in both the cases they are missing.' After a thoughtful pause, UKC asked, 'Do you have the sketches with you?'

Vivek gave the sketches to Neema, who held them in front of UKC. After a while, UKC eyes widened. 'Are you guys stupid?' Both Abhay and Vivek gave him a puzzled look.

'Can't you figure out that the girl in both the sketches is the same? Just look at her eyes!'

Neema gave the sketches back to the police officers. They looked at them intently. And suddenly realized that UKC was right! The girl in the two sketches was the same. The men, however, didn't look similar to each other.

'I didn't look that closely. And these aren't pictures. Mere sketches based on someone's description. Moreover, it was a task getting the sketches made from Sharma's parents' narrations,' Abhay said.

'Spare me the excuses. I'm not your boss. In fact, I'm sure you haven't shown Tandon and his sister's sketches to Singh, or Mishra and her sister's sketches to Mrs Basu.'

Abhay nodded.

'Do that immediately and let me know what their reactions are. I want the reactions to be recorded. I don't trust you people. I never did.'

Abhay looked down. He knew it had been a stupid mistake.

'Let's watch Mrs Vishwanath's video,' UKC said. The video was played, her response time was recorded. After it ended, UKC took a while before saying, 'I think this one is different. The same people might be involved in the other two cases.'

'So Mrs Vishwanath cannot be a suspect?' Abhay asked.

'There's nothing that connects her husband's incident with the other two. If you want you can probe it as a separate case. But I want you to show Mrs Vishwanath the other two sketches as well. Who knows maybe she has seen them somewhere. We shouldn't leave loose ends.'

'I agree.' Abhay said.

'Do you suspect either of the two women?' Vivek asked.

'Both Mrs Basu and Singh have motives. Whether they were strong enough to act upon them is debatable. And nothing can be said till we solve the mystery behind this brother–sister duo. I'm cent per cent sure that Erina Tandon and Priyanshi Mishra are one and the same girl. But what about Kunal Mishra and Nihit Tandon?'

'So, we still don't have a specific suspect?' It was Vivek again.

'Right now, if you bring me a mirror, I might even suspect the person I see in the reflection,' UKC laughed. 'Just kidding,' he added.

4

An anxious Dhrithi was driving towards Faridabad.

That morning, after reaching the police station, Dhrithi had realized that the other two, Kashvi and Sanisha, had also been summoned along with her. But they were taken into a room, one at a time, just like it had happened on the interrogation day. Dhrithi didn't know about the other two, but she was trying to hire a lawyer even though she was not yet a suspect in her husband's case. So far she had cooperated with the police. She had taken leave from office. She was yet to tell her in-laws that she was a working woman. Initially, when Satyam was admitted to the ICU, his parents and brother had come to Delhi. Now, only his parents were staying with Dhrithi.

She couldn't believe her eyes when she was shown the four sketches. The girl looked more or less like Ananya. But while Nihit resembled Kshay, she couldn't say the same for Kunal as the latter had a big beard and thick hair. Moreover, his sketch wasn't very clear. But why would these two be involved with Kashvi, Sanisha or her? There was no apparent reason that she could figure out. It was then that the thought struck her—she had better confirm if Kshay was really dead.

That could be the reason why Nihit and Kunal were absconding, that is if they and Kshay were one and the same person. For that she needed a phone number and a place that wouldn't be tracked back to her. So, it was Faridabad. She had saved the number of the Goa beach resort from the Internet. She stopped at the first PCO she spotted in Faridabad. It was next to a rundown shop. A knot of men was busy arguing over something outside the shop. Dhrithi swallowed nervously as she got out of her car and went to use the phone. Thankfully, it was working. She dialed the Goa resort. A man picked up.

'Hi, I wanted to know if there was any death in your resort a month ago?' The moment she uttered the words, she realized how shady she sounded.

'Excuse me? Who is this?' the man asked.

'I can't tell you who I am but I need to know if a guest was murdered in one of your villas a month ago?'

'No, ma'am! Nothing of that sort has ever happened here. Who told you such nonsensical things?! Ours is a reputable resort!'

Dhrithi cut the call and got back into her car. Her hands were shaking as she started the engine. Kshay was not dead. It had been a set-up. To corner her. To blackmail her into injecting Satyam with lead. She hit the brakes and broke down. If she hadn't told anyone about Kshay earlier, now she simply couldn't at any cost. She would be directly charged with culpable homicide as she had no alibi. How would she prove that she was having an affair with Kshay? *Unless the police caught the woman who had said she was Ananya and the man who had said he was Kshay, and made them confess*, Dhrithi thought. And the scenes of Kshay fucking her brains out in the Neemrana hotel room, his studio and in Goa flashed before her. Dhrithi smacked the steering wheel hard and screamed in frustration and anxiety.

UKC was with Neema. She was helping him drink his Scotch on the rocks. This was his favourite time of the day. He believed there were only two worthwhile things in life: the human mind and Scotch. With every sip, his mind was digging deeper into the case. And the more he thought about it, the more he got puzzled. If he assumed a killer duo was on the loose, there were glaring loopholes in the cases. When he treated each case exclusively, he couldn't figure out how the same brother and sister figured in both Mr Basu and Satyam Vishwanath's cases. Mrs Vishwanath was clean. Abhay had called Neema and told her to relay the information that Singh had recognized Erina and Nihit Tandon as Priyanshi and perhaps Kunal Mishra, but Mrs Vishwanath hadn't. This meant Satyam Vishwanath's case was exclusive. And yet, he too was in the same ICU with his friends. By his fourth, and final, peg, UKC was sure that either there were layers of information waiting to be peeled off or this was the simplest yet perfect crime that he had always longed for.

As UKC was burning his grey cells to get to the bottom of the case, at another corner of Delhi, Ashvamedha was having steaming-hot meatball noodle soup with Sama for dinner at home.

'How is it?' he asked.

'Perfect. You made it the first time, and yet it's just perfect!' Sama exclaimed.

'Perfection is hyped. People don't talk about what's more important than perfection.'

'What's that?'

'Preparation. Perfection is begotten by preparation. I looked up the recipe, bought whatever was needed, did a beta-run myself last night and here you are now,' he said with a hint of pride.

'Touché!' Sama quipped. She had a bit of the soup and said, 'Did you prepare as much for Kashvi, Dhrithi and Sanisha?'

Ashvamedha didn't answer immediately. He finished his soup, and waited for Sama to finish hers.

'A perfect crime isn't about the way it's done. The preparation, the procedure, of course, is important. But it's also about how you chalk out the plan such that it confuses everyone involved—from the victim, to the fake suspects, to the police. So that nobody can ever come to a definite conclusion.'

'But do you think you have been fair to the women? Especially Sanisha?'

Ashvamedha stayed quiet. He knew every story had that one part which was disturbing.

5

The medical expenses had shot up exponentially for Adhik's family. It had been six weeks since he was admitted to the ICU and the bill had already reached a staggering Rs 21,00,000. Adhik's medical insurance coverage was for Rs 10,00,000. His father had taken care of the rest, but now the family was feeling the pinch.

'Has there been any improvement?' Adhik's father asked the doctor once he was ushered into his cabin.

'I'll be honest with you. I really can't see any way in which we can either improve or revive Adhik. Right now, he is completely on external support. We can wait but I can't guarantee you full recovery. Like Mr Vishwanath's parents, you too can take him to London or any other place with better medical facilities. As far as we are concerned, there's really no hope.'

Adhik's father was a state government employee, slated to retire the next year. He still had to sponsor his daughter's education and marriage.

'What do you suggest, doctor?' he asked.

'I don't think it sounds good but I guess sometimes it's better to accept the situation.'

'What do you mean?'

'Let Adhik off the external support. Trust me, if I'd seen an iota of improvement, I wouldn't have suggested this. I mean, we can keep him here for another month or for that matter many months. But this will only inflate your bill, which might be profitable for us, but will be of no consequence for Adhik.'

Adhik's father's eyes turned moist as he took leave of the doctor. His wife and daughter were waiting outside. Behind them was Sanisha. She was always with them even though they had been consistently ignoring her. He told them what the doctor had said. His wife started howling immediately. A nurse came and asked her to be quiet. Her daughter and husband took her downstairs to the lobby. Although nobody said anything aloud, a decision had been made. They would remove the external support. Sanisha was rooted to her spot. After Adhik's family left, she suddenly felt weak in her knees and sat down heavily on one of the chairs. A month ago she couldn't accept that Adhik had betrayed her. And now, when she knew he would be off the life support soon, she didn't know what to feel, think or say. Her jaws had tightened, her body was warm and eyes moist. Just then, her phone flashed ACP Abhay's name. She didn't pick up. He called again. She finally picked up, but couldn't recognize her own voice when she spoke.

'Sanisha madam, we have court orders for a lie detector test. You have to come to the police station tomorrow at 10 a.m.'

'Okay,' she said and cut the call. It didn't mean anything to her any more.

UKC had insisted on having a lie detector test. He knew that a perfect crime was only a fallacy. There was always a piece of information hidden somewhere, either deliberately or otherwise, which kept authorities from cracking a case. And in these three cases, he had a gut feeling that some information was still being withheld. The questions were simple: who was hiding the information, what was it and why was it being hidden? But UKC had an inkling that the answers would be complicated.

Shweta met Ashvamedha at school and requested him to come to her house. 'Sanisha has locked herself in her room since last night. She is neither opening the door nor listening to anything I'm saying. I think she might listen to you,' Shweta said desperately.

Ashvamedha thought for a moment and said, 'I'll be there.'

Later in the evening, he visited Shweta's house. Sanisha was still inside her room; she had moved out of her old place and was now staying with Shweta and her son. Ashvamedha knocked on the door a couple of times.

'Sanisha, it's me,' he said. A worried Shweta was hovering close at hand. Seconds later, the door unlocked. Ashvamedha turned to look at Shweta. She gestured him to go inside. As he went inside, she softly closed the door from outside.

'What happened?' Ashvamedha asked Sanisha. He had never seen her that distressed or defeated before. She never came across as someone who could be beaten.

'They are pulling the plug off Adhik day after tomorrow,' she said resignedly. The reality was still seeping in. Ashvamedha stood with his back against the wall.

'You know,' she said, 'when I learnt he wasn't going to marry me, stand by me any more, I promised myself I wouldn't let this experience or anything related to him affect me or break me down. But I've only cried ever since. I've understood, and surprisingly so, that we women are incorrigible. No matter what our man does to us, if anything happens to him, we always wither away in pain. We might distance ourselves from the relationship, but its essence will always remain as seeds inside us, always with the potential of growing back into feelings that can shake our whole world.'

'You still love him?' he asked.

'No. I don't. But I care for him. And that, I don't think, will ever go.' She sighed and said, 'What do you do when life makes you hate the person who once meant the world to you only to be followed by his death?'

'The end or the beginning isn't in our hands. Only the choices we make during the journey are. Or at least it seems so when it's happening. I don't think Adhik deserved you. I don't think you deserved him either,' Ashvamedha said.

'Now, it's beyond who deserved whom. If Adhik was alive, I would have asked him to apologize and then get lost. Now I feel guilty over the last fight we had. I feel guilty over everything. Funnily enough, I even feel that I was harsh on him, even though it was he who had betrayed me. He should've been the guilty one. But now he is dead . . .'

A few minutes went by. Neither spoke.

'I know perhaps the police will arrest me on the basis of circumstantial evidence. That will certainly bring peace to his parents, for whom I'm a witch who ate their son. They won't be able to take him abroad like Satyam or Parth's parents. So their redemption lies in my trial.' A moment later, she looked at Ashvamedha and asked, 'Do you think I should lie that I was the one driving the car? That I killed Adhik? That I can't take it any more. That my life, anyway, is over. Neither are my parents going to accept me nor anyone else in Bhopal. If I stay in Delhi, this guilt will eat me away steadily.'

Ashvamedha walked up to her and placed his palm over her head. 'You haven't done anything wrong. You'll be safe.'

'How do you know I'll be safe?'

'Trust me.'

Sanisha put her arms around his waist. And hugging him, she cried her heart out.

Abhay had some official work so it was Inspector Vivek who brought the lie detector test results to UKC. Neema helped him go through them. The moment he was done, he cracked up.

'Wow! This case only becomes weirder and weirder. The ones with strong motives to kill their partners passed the test.' He was talking about Kashvi and Sanisha. 'But the one who had no apparent motive has failed at it.' It was Dhrithi.

'Even Abhay sir and I were talking about the same thing,' Vivek said.

'Since when did Tandon come into Mrs Basu's life?' UKC asked Neema.

'Around six months ago,' she said. Vivek would have been surprised had Abhay not told him that Neema was UKC's back-up hard drive. No information ever escaped her.

'Get me Dhrithi Vishwanath's mobile phone records for the past six months.'

'May I know why, sir? I'm curious.' Vivek asked.

'Chances are, a brother–sister duo entered her life as well. I'm sure of it. What I'm not sure is why Dhrithi has been hiding it.'

'Hmm.' Vivek stood up to leave.

'Any progress on Nihit and Erina Tandon or Priyanshi and Kunal Mishra?' UKC asked.

'Not yet,' Abhay said.

'If Delhi Police can't hunt down a man and a woman, then they should shove their faces up their own asses.'

6

'I'm thinking of quitting my job,' Ashvamedha said as he finished checking the copies of his students for the night. Unit tests were on and there was a lot of pressure at work. But that was not why he wanted to resign.

'Why so?' Sama asked. She was reading a book.

'I don't see any future for these kids. Times have changed, people's desires, ambitions, outlooks, aspirations, almost everything has become mediocre. It has taken such deep root within us. Mediocrity, our gullibility towards technology and the inability to remain objective about anything. Believe me, these are the factors that will puncture us like nothing before. The end will be real bad. Worse than our beginnings. I'm glad neither you nor I will stay alive to witness it.'

There was no response from Sama. He saw her put her book down.

'What happened?' he asked.

'I was thinking about Sanisha. Based on whatever you've told me, I think somewhere you've wronged her.'

'I did something, which had certain implications. She is a victim of those implications more than anything else. I never intentionally tried to hurt her.'

'I know you didn't but if you analyze carefully, Kashvi fell for something and made a choice. So did Dhrithi. They shouldn't have fallen for whatever they did in the first place. But with Sanisha it was different. It was Adhik who was responsible for screwing up their lives.'

'What's your point?'

'Can anything be done to save her?'

Ashvamedha stared at Sama for some time.

'You really want me to do something to save her?'

'Can you?'

'I can.'

'Then you should.'

'All right,' he said softly, after a pensive pause.

UKC also asked for call records of Kashvi and Sanisha for the past six months. They didn't find any suspicious number on Sanisha's list. Kashvi had stored Nihit and Erina's numbers. *But she didn't talk to Nihit as much as someone who was having an affair with another person would*, UKC noted. It was Dhrithi's phone records that threw up problems. There were two numbers whose owners weren't linked with her. She was summoned to the police station where, after a little pressure, Dhrithi finally confessed to everything.

'It belongs to Kshay Rawat. And the other number is of his business partner, Ananya. They run a company called Social Keeda. They got in touch with me and I hired them as my social media managers. But then, I got into a physical relationship with Kshay. Nobody knew about it. It was all going smoothly till we went for a day-long trip to Goa. There, I found him in a pool of blood in our resort room. Later, a video of it was sent to me. I was blackmailed by an anonymous person into injecting three syringes of lead either into myself or Satyam.'

'And she, like a dutiful wife, chose her husband over herself,' UKC said after watching Dhrithi's confession video. 'The interesting part is,' he continued, 'that she was given two choices. But whoever gave her those options knew she wasn't going to inject herself. Hobson's Choice, as it's called.'

'Can we be sure?' Abhay asked.

'The first rule in solving any crime case is to look at everything objectively. And question. Last night, I was thinking that we were going the way we were made to by the culprits. And now, after watching this confession, I'm sure of one thing.'

'Which is?'

'The women weren't the targets. They were the means. The men were the target.'

'The brother and sister came into the women's lives because their husbands were the targets?' Abhay sounded incredulous.

'I don't know how many people are behind this and why but I think I've cracked one thing. This brother and sister duo planted motives in the women against their husbands. They introduced themselves as Nihit and Erina Tandon to Kashvi Basu, taking advantage of her obsession with social media to instigate her against her husband. It's like a third person playing a game of chess with two people. It's just that the players think it's their partner who is the opponent. And finally, it was checkmate for both Parth and Kashvi Basu.

In Dhrithi Vishwanath's case, her unfulfilled sexual need and social media aspiration were used to bring her to a point where she would do what the culprits wanted her to, but in a way that she would be the one responsible for injecting her husband. It's again a checkmate situation. While in Sanisha Singh's case, it's different. I'm sure there is a reason behind this difference but I haven't figured it out yet. This time, the tool that was used was marriage. Both her statements and call records prove that Kunal Mishra approached her only after she had moved out of the house in which she lived with Adhik. Only one phone call was made to her to call her to the mall parking lot. You have checked Adhik Sharma's phone records. He too got a call from the same number, two minutes before Sanisha Singh had been called from that number. It was a set-up. I bet her car was driven by the person, or persons, who is/are responsible for this plan.'

There was pin-drop silence. Everyone was still digesting what UKC had said.

'Till now, I'd only heard of toying with witnesses and planting cues to confuse the police. Here, even the motives have been planted in people's minds to misguide us and them. Do we understand what a brilliant mind we are dealing with here?' UKC sounded excited. 'Now I know why the police couldn't catch him or them yet.'

The last bit was unnecessary, Abhay thought.

'So, what do we have now?' he asked aloud.

'Sanisha Singh is clean. Mrs Vishwanath isn't. We aren't so sure about Mrs Basu either. She could have helped Nihit Tandon kill Parth Basu or perhaps it was Tandon himself who tried to kill him. But we don't have either Tandon or Basu to help us out here.'

'We can tell Sanisha that she is free to travel outside Delhi,' Vivek said.

'Why, where did she want to go?' UKC asked.

'She wanted to go to Bhopal. Her home town.'

'I would say it's fine but get a tracker to follow her for some time. Who knows, keeping oneself clean could be the tool she used to commit the crime.'

'You are saying Sanisha Singh could be in cahoots with this brother and sister duo?' Vivek asked.

'I'm saying God has given us a brain. And he has also given us a dick.' UKC glanced askance at Neema. 'Excuse the language.' He looked at Vivek, 'Why do we use one a little too much and the other a little too less?'

Vivek looked offended.

'I hope my joke didn't poke you,' UKC said.

'We must leave now,' Abhay said, standing up. 'I think we have almost cracked the case.'

'Not till we nab this duo.'

'Do you believe what Dhrithi Vishwanath said? About the death of the man named Kshay Rawat when she left the Goa resort?' Abhay asked, and continued, 'The airlines have corroborated her story. One Kshay Rawat and Dhrithi Vishwanath did travel on that date to Goa. They did spend time at the resort together. Only Rawat's name is registered there, but a woman can't lie about such a thing, especially when it involves her modesty. And the sketch she made of Jain and Rawat . . .'

'Without doubt they are the same duo: Erina–Nihit, Ananya–Kshay and Priyanshi–Kunal,' Vivek chipped in.

'What are you doing about it?' UKC asked.

'We are at it. After senior Dr Basu saw the sketches, he talked to the commissioner. There is immense pressure to crack the case. A major manhunt is on. I'm sure we will nab this brother–sister duo soon.'

'Sometimes I think the entire system is like shit. We don't work without any pressure,' UKC said.

Abhay and Vivek exchanged looks, abusing UKC in their minds.

Sanisha couldn't believe it when she was informed by ACP Abhay that she could travel within India for the time being. She didn't know if it were Adhik's parents who had taken their case back or the police had figured out that she was innocent. She did visit her old flat, where Adhik's parents were now staying. A van was parked outside to take Adhik to Agra, his home town, where his last rites were to be performed. Sanisha wanted to be there but knew that although his parents hadn't objected to her presence in the hospital, they would most definitely do so in Agra as their family members would be there.

She went straight to Shweta's school to meet Ashvamedha, but found out that Ashvamedha was on sick leave. After a little bit of pestering, she got his address from the school office. It was high time she met Sama. Sanisha made her way to old Delhi and took some time to locate his house. It looked a little decrepit. In fact, it didn't even look occupied. She pressed a dusty doorbell. Ashvamedha opened the door.

For the first time, Ashvamedha looked as if he had been taken by surprise.

'I got your address from the school. Hope I'm not disturbing?'

'Not at all. Sama and I were having tea. Come in,' he said. She stepped inside. He closed the door after her. Sanisha left within fifteen minutes. And after turning a corner, she vomited her guts out. She couldn't believe what she had seen at Ashvamedha's place. Even the last two months had not prepared her for it. *Not for this*, she thought. She could hear her heart beat faster every moment and bile rise up in her throat.

7

ACP Abhay was sipping his tea while sitting in Dr Samaresh Kumar Basu's office. It was a newly made office for his political endeavors. Abhay had come to brief him about the case. He told him about the manhunt.

'We are certain that this man, Nihit Tandon, or whatever his real name is, attacked and fatally wounded your son, Parth. But what we aren't certain about is whether Mrs Basu is an accomplice or not. She has stuck to her statement that the man in the photograph is Nihit Tandon but that she never had a relationship with him. Our guess is that Mrs Basu might have known about the attack but we are not sure. We are also yet to prove if your son and Erina Tandon were having an affair. He never called her.'

Dr Basu looked pensive. Other than Abhay, only his manager was there in the room. He looked at him. Abhay realized the glance was meant for the manager to think out loud. He seemed to be a trusted man.

'I think,' the manager said, 'we should arrest Kashvi on the charge of being in cahoots with the man who attacked Parth.'

Abhay couldn't help but throw an incredulous look at him. The manager shrugged and continued: 'Kashvi should be locked up for a month. That should give you enough time to catch this man and his sister. If he confesses that Kashvi is telling the truth, you can release her or else we'll let the law take its course.'

A smile appeared on Dr Basu's face. Abhay had clearly missed the point but senior Basu had understood it. He looked at the manager and said, 'Masterstroke! This way the people of my constituency will think here's a man who doesn't take soft stands. "He didn't even spare his daughter-in-law, unflinchingly handed her over to the police." They will believe I am an honest man who holds his principles and ideals more dearly than his family members.' A tinge of self-pride was already shining on his face.

'Precisely my point, sir. And we can immediately shift Parth baba to London,' the manager said.

Abhay had come across a lot of people in his job. But Dr Basu had to take the cake when it came to having a chameleon personality. Never before had he met a man who so ruthlessly took advantage of his son's misfortune and used his daughter-in-law as a pawn to further his political agenda.

'Finally we have a solution to this, ACP,' Dr Basu said.

'Right, sir. I'll get an arrest warrant for Kashvi Basu,' Abhay said.

'Good.' Dr Basu turned to his manager and said, 'Get a press release ready for this. Frame everything in a way that the public sympathizes with my son and me. Also, inform Kashvi's parents. Assure them that she will be out in a month. This is only a courtesy call. They won't like it, but given my position and power, they won't be able to say much either.'

'Right, sir,' the manager said and left, along with Abhay.

Dhrithi had already been taken into custody after her confession. Her in-laws were shocked at the revelation. Satyam's father wanted to file another case, but his brother advised him against it. He said it was more important to shift Satyam to London. The law anyway wouldn't spare Dhrithi now that she had confessed. Sitting in the lock-up, and soon to be transferred to jail, Dhrithi could hear her Nanna and Satyam laughing at her condition. As if they knew what was going to happen to her from the very beginning. *Good girls don't end up in jail*, they kept telling her. There was no way she could mute them. Their allegations were gnawing at her conscience. She could do nothing. The police had cornered her into squeezing out the confession. And with it, she knew her life was over. Her mother-in-law had cursed her after the family learnt how their son had been poisoned. And those curses, Dhrithi knew, would be her only friends during the rest of her life. The kind of friends who didn't let you live. Or die either.

Sanisha learnt about Dhrithi's arrest from ACP Abhay, soon after Dhrithi stopped responding to her messages. But there was something that was disturbing her much more. What she'd seen at Ashvamedha's place had stayed with her. Every time she remembered it, a chill ran down her spine. *It just can't be true*, she kept thinking. She didn't know how to behave when Ashvamedha came to teach Shweta's son at home. The only thing she asked him was, 'Where does Sama work?' She tried to sound as casual as possible.

'HDFC bank, Janakpuri branch. Why do you ask?' he said. Till then, Sanisha had given Ashvamedha the benefit of doubt by being in denial. But with his answer she knew she wasn't talking to the Ashvamedha she knew at college. This was someone who needed help. But how would she put it across to him?

'Oh, I had some bank work . . . at some other bank, I mean. I was wondering if Sama worked there . . . so she could have helped me . . . Actually, I'm leaving for Bhopal soon and wanted to close my bank accounts in Delhi.' She only hoped he would fall for this stupid excuse.

'I see.' He didn't say anything more and left to teach the kid.

The next day, Sanisha went to HDFC bank, Janakpuri, and met the branch manager.

'I want to know about Sama Akhtar. She is supposedly working here.'

The branch manager was new. She introduced Sanisha to an executive who knew Sama.

'Of course, Sama ma'am worked here. But she has been absconding from work for a year and a half now,' the executive said.

'Absconding?' Sanisha couldn't hide her surprise.

'Well, one fine day she stopped coming to office. We called her, tried to get in touch with her husband, but nothing happened. We had to declare her "absconding". Her accounts were frozen but nobody came to claim the money.'

'May I get her home address? Not the Delhi one,' Sanisha said.

'Sure. If you manage to reach her, please ask her to get in touch with us urgently. She was such a nice and warm woman. I don't know what happened to her. Nobody in this branch can forget the shaami kebabs she used to bring for us.' There was genuine concern and respect for Sama on the executive's face.

'Sure,' Sanisha said. Sama's permanent address said she was from Kakori, Uttar Pradesh. There was a landline number as well. She called up the number but no one picked up. Sanisha then booked a flight ticket to Lucknow, from where she decided to take a cab to Kakori. She was working on a hunch, and not a plan. All she wanted to know was whether Ashvamedha had told her the truth about Sama and himself.

She stayed at a friend's place in Lucknow for the night and took a cab the next morning to Kakori. It was afternoon by the time she reached Sama's house. It was a rambling old bungalow that looked ready to collapse at any moment. She pressed the doorbell only to realize it was out of order. She banged on the door. A ten-year-old boy opened the door.

'Do you have anyone older in the house?' she asked. The boy ran inside and came back accompanied by a woman.

'Namaste, my name is Sanisha Singh. I've come from Delhi. Actually, I knew Sama in college.'

The woman's expression changed on hearing Sama's name. She ushered Sanisha inside and introduced herself as Sama's brother's wife. It was Sama's father who later told her everything.

'Initially, we weren't happy about getting her married into another community, but when she introduced Ashvamedha to us, we thought he was a good man. Someone who would take care of Sama and happily make the adjustments required in an interfaith marriage. We got her married to him.

She used to come here with Ashvamedha every Eid. And that year was no different.'

'Which year?' Sanisha asked.

'2016. They were coming to Kakori by train. She'd called us from the train as well. But they never came home.'

'What do you mean?' Sanisha asked nervously.

'It took us ten days to get in touch with Ashvamedha since the call from the train. He told us Sama was missing. He said he had filed a police complaint.'

'Did you meet him after that?'

'I didn't as Ashvamedha never came here. But one of my sons, Afzal, met him in Delhi. Sama was still missing. He told us how depressed Ashvamedha was.'

'And then . . . ?'

'She is still alive in our prayers. I don't know what happened to my daughter, but I hope Allah isn't this cruel to us. She will come back. I don't know when or from where but she will.' Sama's father broke down. Sanisha had tears in her eyes but remained steely. Soon after, she took her leave not knowing if she should meet Ashvamedha again or not.

As her cab drove off from Sama's house, another cab, which had been following her, too turned on its engine. Inspector Vivek was in it. He had been following her from New Delhi to Lucknow to Kakori.

8

While Inspector Vivek was following Sanisha, ACP Abhay finally got to what had eluded him for so long. Standing in front of UKC's house, he had never felt more victorious. He took a deep breath and went inside.

When Neema wheeled a grumpy-looking UKC into the room, Abhay knew why he was annoyed. Rarely did a case go on for this long with UKC. His last challenging case was solved within twenty days. This one had gone on for three months now.

'This had better be good,' UKC said.

'It indeed is!' Abhay said.

A few seconds went by.

'And for whom or what are we waiting for?' UKC said drily.

'I'm sorry. So, we've located the brother and sister,' Abhay said with a hint of pride.

'When? Where and who are they?' UKC's eyes grew bigger behind his high-power specs.

'A family in Kosli, in Rewari district of Haryana, has finally claimed to know the girl. Her real name is Rashmi Rathi. They showed a photograph of hers. She used make-up to look different every time.'

'And the man?' UKC asked.

'I'll come to him in a bit. Rashmi is actually twenty-one years old. A music video was shot in Kosli. Rashmi, who had always been interested in films, visited the set with her friend. There, one of the still photographers, Akshay Bhatnagar, fell in love with her. Bhatnagar is our man. They aren't siblings; they're lovers!' Abhay noticed he had UKC's unflinching attention. He continued, 'After the music video was shot, Bhatnagar kept coming back to Kosli every weekend from Delhi, where he worked. He is actually from Gwalior. We have checked with his parents. He has two younger sisters; one in the first year of college and the other in school. The parents genuinely don't know where he has been for the last five months. He last met them a year ago and last called them six months ago, when he told them he was going somewhere far off. He said he would leave some money for them. He transferred Rs 5,00,000 to his parents' account. But he had himself credited the money to his own account a day before transferring it to his parents. Also, the account hasn't been used since then. Which is about four months now. We've cross-checked all of it. It's true.' Abhay paused.

'Tell me more about Rathi and him. Since when did they fall in love?' UKC said, sensing the actual story was set in Kosli.

'2017. As I said, Bhatnagar visited Kosli often and their love grew. But Rashmi knew her family wouldn't accept Bhatnagar as he was from a different community. Her family was also not happy that Bhatnagar was a photographer, an occupation they understood little about and frowned upon.

They thought he would abandon their daughter later. Then one day, Rashmi agreed to get married to whoever her parents wanted her to. But she wished to do a computer course for six months in Delhi first. The family was apprehensive initially but agreed as one of her brothers stayed in Delhi and ran a gym. He was her local guardian.'

'And these six months were the last six months,' UKC said.

'Exactly! They don't know where she is currently. The last time they heard from her was three months ago. Her brother had called her. We took the number but got no lead from it. They didn't lodge an official complaint, fearing their reputation might be affected among the townspeople.'

'Their reputation is more important to them than their daughter. Wow! Did I tell you, Neema, that I've no expectations from humans?' UKC turned towards Neema. She nodded imperceptibly.

'They last heard from her three months ago. Six months ago she demanded to pursue a course. Bhatnagar told his parents he is going somewhere far away. He had transferred the money during this period. So, it's clear there was some plan. And the plan involved the three couples. You know the first thing that is locked when someone plans something?' UKC asked Neema. She nodded.

'The result. It's a plan if the desired result is locked. They wanted the three friends—Parth, Satyam and Adhik—to die. Why? How are they related to these three couples?' UKC was talking to himself.

'We checked with everyone involved in the case. Nobody has any link to Kosli or Gwalior. Or for that matter with Rashmi or Bhatnagar. Nobody knew them,' Abhay chipped in.

UKC turned glum again. As if the ray of hope that he had just seen had now disappeared.

'What if I ask you to look for me now?' UKC suddenly asked Abhay.

For a moment, Abhay didn't know what that meant. And then he answered, 'Here you are, sitting in front of us.'

'Good. Neema, take me inside.' Neema wheeled UKC out of the living room and into the corridor leading to the bedroom. Abhay was about to leave when he heard UKC say, 'Now look for me in the living room.'

'Of course, you are not here,' Abhay said, feeling slightly irritated.

Neema wheeled him back into the room. 'I hope my joke didn't poke you,' UKC said. Abhay didn't respond.

'You didn't find me because I wasn't here. Either Bhatnagar and Rashmi are dead or they left the country after executing their plans, before any official complaints were registered. And my gut feeling says they must have used fake names and identities.' UKC sounded conclusive. And every time he sounded like that, Abhay knew, he would be right. His phone rang. He talked for a few minutes and then cut the call.

'We've got to know something else. Although we are not sure if it's related to the case,' Abhay told UKC. His stare told him he should continue.

'Vivek was following Singh like you had wanted. First, she visited a friend's house in old Delhi, then she went to this friend's wife's workplace in Janakpuri and then to her house in Kakori, UP. Vivek asked around and found out that this woman, her friend's wife, has been missing for the past year and a half. I think it's a different case. We can get another team to . . .'

'What's the friend's name?'

'One Ashvamedha Chauhaan.'

'Find out if he is related to the cases. If he is, then let me know immediately. Else forget about it for the time being.'

'Right,' Abhay said and left.

Seven hours later, he called up UKC. He sounded excited.

'We did a background check on Chauhaan,' he said.

'And . . . ?'

'He pursued his MBA along with Parth Basu, Adhik Sharma, Sanisha Singh, Satyam and Dhrithi Vishwanath from the same institute. He was expelled from college and later completed his course from some other institution. Subsequently, he worked on a summer project with Parth, Adhik and Satyam two years ago. However, he left the project midway.'

UKC had only three words: 'Raid his place. Now!'

'At it!' Abhay said. For a change, UKC and he were thinking on the same lines. In the next one hour, police reached Ashvamedha's place. They realized he wasn't at home. They broke in.

A minute into the house Abhay shouted, '*Kya hai yeh sab, behenchod?*'

9

Abhay and his team were inside the house when they heard someone's footsteps outside. They took their positions. The moment Ashvamedha entered, they leapt on him. He tried to fight them off but was outnumbered and soon pinned to the ground.

'Tell us what you know, else we know how to make you cooperate!' Abhay barked at him.

Ashvamedha calmed down. Then he looked at Sama and said, 'I hope they didn't disturb you.'

That was when Abhay realized what was wrong. He asked a constable to stay behind while the others dragged Ashvamedha out to the police jeep. He was handcuffed and shoved inside. Onlookers had gathered in the lane; they looked baffled. Never in their wildest dreams had they thought that a man like Ashvamedha would be whisked away by the police one day. Nobody ever had any complaints against him in the locality.

Sanisha heard of Ashvamedha's arrest from Inspector Vivek. He'd asked her to visit the police station because of her connection with Ashvamedha. When she reached there, she was asked to identify a man. She couldn't look at him for more than a few seconds. His eyebrows had split and he had blood on his face; his face was swollen. The man was in his underwear and had welts all over his body, probably from caning, she guessed.

'Do you know him?' Inspector Vivek asked roughly.

'No!' Sanisha answered confidently as she sat opposite him.

'That's Ashvamedha Chauhaan,' he said. She didn't believe him when he took his name. Then she looked closely at the man. It indeed was Ashvamedha! The man she had idolized since college. The man whose name brought a twinkle in her eyes. Looking at him now, she had tears in her eyes.

'Oh my God! What have you people done to him?' Sanisha couldn't help but cry.

'He is innocent. I'm sure he hasn't done anything. You don't have the right to beat up someone without any reason!' she said, feeling helpless.

Inspector Vivek spoke grimly after a thoughtful pause, 'Why would an innocent man live with a dead body for a year and a half? We talked to Sama Akhtar's family. Her father said she had been missing for the same time. I'm sure he will confess his crime soon.'

Sanisha glanced at him. She knew he wasn't lying. When she'd gone to Ashvamedha's place, she had seen what looked like a body propped up on the bed. The reality had been so disturbing—Ashvamedha had been talking to Sama as if she was alive—that she went into denial. Sanisha kept telling herself that he couldn't have killed her. Even now, she believed that he could never have killed his wife.

Ashvamedha loved Sama the way a woman can only hope to be loved by a man, she thought.

'We called you because we know you knew this man and his wife. Her family members have been informed,' Vivek said.

'I know him. We studied together.'

'We shall record whatever you know about them. So hold on to the information as of now. I'll set up a video session in some time,' Vivek said and then asked Sanisha to wait.

'Can I talk to him?' she asked.

'Sure. But I think he has become unconscious now.' Vivek motioned a constable to open the lock-up. Her knees shivering, Sanisha stepped inside gingerly. The evening she had spotted him at the school months ago flashed in front of her eyes. He had lied so confidently about Sama. He seemed . . . happy, contented. There was no way she could've guessed that he wasn't well. But what had made him live with her body for so long? How did Sama die? Sanisha wanted to caress his forehead, but was repulsed by the blood and sweat. Instead she asked gently, 'Ashva . . .' but there was no response. The man she had loved so purely was half-dead in front of her. The man she had always respected had turned out to have had a dark secret. Thinking that he wouldn't regain his senses any time soon, she turned to leave when she heard him murmur.

'They shouldn't have touched her.' Seconds later he passed out again. Inspector Vivek told her the video session had been set up. Sanisha was asked to tell them whatever she knew about Ashvamedha and Sama, and whatever she had found out at Kakori. Sanisha realized she'd been followed, which made her feel guilty. *Maybe she had led them to Ashvamedha? But it had to happen one day*, she thought and followed Vivek to the interrogation room.

Sanisha's video was shown to UKC. This time, only Inspector Vivek was visiting him.

'Abhay sir knows it's a different case altogether, with no apparent links to the ones we had approached you for, but he still wanted you to see the video as it involves Sanisha Singh, who was once a suspect in Adhik Sharma's case.'

'Did Ashvamedha say why he was living with his wife's body for so long? What does the post-mortem report say?' UKC asked.

'We are awaiting the report but as the body is in an advanced stage of decomposition. I don't think the autopsy will be of much help. All that we do know is that he had plastered the entire body except the face and the feet. That kept it going without stink,' Vivek said.

'Do you think he knows more than he has said?'

'He has said nothing except, "They shouldn't have touched her." I'm sure he knows more. We thrashed him for a good two hours, then stopped, fearing he might die in custody.'

'What do Sama Akhtar's family members have to say?'

'Her brother was at the police station. He said they'd heard from her a year and a half ago when she'd called from the Shramjeevi Superfast Express. We looked up that date. Sama Akhtar and Ashvamedha Chauhaan were on the passenger list and were supposed to get down at Lucknow that night.'

'And they don't reach Lucknow. He tells her family she has gone missing and that he has lodged a missing complaint.' UKC's tone was analytical.

'He didn't lodge any complaint though. I checked,' Vivek said.

There was silence. Vivek understood UKC was thinking hard as the latter's eyes were darting from left to right.

'Use the truth serum, extract a confession and get done with the case. Who knows, he might have killed her himself and decided to live with the body. Humans have such weird fetishes! That's why I hate them. Any leads on Bhatnagar and Rathi?'

'Not yet,' Vivek said. Neema started to wheel UKC out of the room. He stood up and said, 'The usage of the truth serum is unethical.'

'Tell Abhay I suggested it. You can have it done without anyone knowing. If it helps someone confess something and saves lives and time, then I don't see what is so unethical about it. The court might not accept any "under the influence" confession but at least the police might land across some vital information. Then you can decide how to nail him or figure out if he is guilty.'

Abhay, once Vivek reported to him, decided to go ahead with UKC's advice. Ashvamedha was taken to a medical college, where he was injected with sodium pentothal or the truth serum under the supervision of a doctor. He was the police's go-to doctor whenever they wanted to use the procedure and keep it a secret. The process lasted for about five hours. The first thing Abhay did after coming out of the room was call UKC.

'During the test, Ashvamedha Chauhaan took Parth Basu, Adhik Sharma and Satyam Vishwanath's names.' He couldn't hide his excitement. On the other end, UKC heaved a sigh of relief. Finally, the dots were connecting. *No crime, after all, is that perfect*, he thought as he waited impatiently to know the details.

10

Sanisha was on her way home from the NGO when she saw her father's name flashing on the phone. She picked it up immediately.

'Hello, Papa,' she said. For a moment, she wished she could turn back time and become a child again so her father could rescue her from all troubles. But his response brought her back to reality cruelly.

'I'm giving you one week. Either shift to Bhopal or forget us completely!' he said and cut the call. He didn't have to tell her what would happen if she chose to come back. She reached Shweta's place and started packing. She booked a flight ticket to Bhopal for the day after. *If I have to resign myself to fate*, she thought, *then it had better be quick.*

The next morning, news of Kashvi's arrest made national headlines. She couldn't believe her in-laws had decided to turn her in without any evidence. She called up Dhrithi but her phone was switched off. Sanisha went to meet Kashvi at Tihar Jail later that day. She was expecting her to break down but Kashvi seemed to be on a different trip altogether. The first thing she asked for was her mobile phone. Sanisha tried giving it to her but wasn't allowed.

She asked Sanisha to open her Instagram profile. Since her arrest, Kashvi hadn't been able to check her phone as it had been confiscated. She found, through Sanisha, that her followers had reduced by 1 lakh in the last five hours. Kashvi gave Sanisha her user ID and password and told her to deactivate her profile.

'I'm here only for the next one month,' she said. 'After that, I will be released. I can always make a fresh start after that.'

'What about Parth?' Sanisha asked.

'He is being taken to a London hospital, along with Satyam. I'm sure they will be all right there. And I'll be free,' Kashvi said, emphasizing the last word.

Sanisha understood that Kashvi was trying very hard to convince herself. She seemed completely in denial of the present situation. She wanted to ask Kashvi more but knew it wasn't the right time. A phone call with ACP Abhay had made her guess why she had been thrown into jail so suddenly. Talking to her about Ashvamedha was pointless.

'I'm not sure if Dhrithi would be released though. She is in the same jail. Did you know she actually poisoned Satyam?' Kashvi said, sounding vindictive. As if she had finally scored above Dhrithi once and for all.

Sanisha frowned. She didn't know about her arrest. She had wanted to meet Dhrithi as well but learnt from the authorities that the latter had refused to meet anyone. She'd asked for a lawyer to fight her case. She still maintained that she was the one who had injected Satyam with the lethal dose of lead but hadn't done it out of her free will.

She was blackmailed into it. The trial was scheduled in the next couple of days. Sanisha did go to the police station to meet Ashvamedha one last time, but she couldn't enter the building. She knew the sight of him all chained up and beaten would affect her profoundly. She couldn't bear to see her *hero* like that. A day later she left for Bhopal.

A week after that, UKC was shown Ashvamedha's interrogation videos. Since the truth serum test, the police had rained blows on every part of his body to squeeze out information. At the end of the fourth day, he said, 'You can break my body, but you won't be able to touch my soul.' And when he was shown the sketches of Bhatnagar and Rathi, he claimed to not know them.

'I've never seen them.'

On the fifth day, he said, 'Yes. There was a girl and a boy who worked for me. But as I said, I didn't see them so I don't know who they are.'

The beating continued for two more days. 'Yes. It was all a plan to hurt those three bastards. But you won't ever be able to prove it.'

As the interrogation continued and the videos piled up, even UKC felt that his patience was being tested. He kept replaying the videos, especially going back to a particular line that Ashvamedha had said.

There was a girl and a boy who worked for me but as I said, I didn't see them.

Suddenly, one day, UKC said, 'Neema, would you please clap for me?' She did as requested. Abhay and Vivek, who were at UKC's place then, exchanged looks.

'What?' UKC asked, noticing the looks exchanged between the officers. 'Don't you still get it? Sometimes the truth is so obvious that we can't accept it. Ashvamedha Chauhaan is telling us the truth. He didn't see the girl and the boy!'

'I'm sure he did,' Abhay said.

'That's where you are missing the brilliance of this man. Doesn't matter what happens to these cases or to him, but I will sure as heckfire remember him! He intentionally didn't see their faces. How exactly he convinced them or transacted with them will be revealed when he chooses to confess. Or maybe another truth serum session will prove useful. But no such session can push him into describing Bhatnagar and Rathi. Normally, we confess something only because we know about it. But what if we don't? Suppose I never saw Inspector Vivek, then would you be able to make me confess how he looks? Ashvamedha made the duo work for him, for reasons I hope we get to know soon, but he never met them so as to never know what they looked like. Brilliant!'

Abhay had rarely seen UKC admiring anybody or anything. But even his jaws dropped hearing UKC's interpretation of Ashvamedha's statement. The scary part was that it was logical.

'What do you suggest we do now?' Abhay asked.

'You will have to break him down for the confession— why did he make Bhatnagar and Rathi do what they did? Why such an elaborate plan? Why did he try to kill those three men? Why did he call them bastards? And what connects Sama Akhtar's death with these men and the couples? And above all . . .'

Abhay and Vivek both braced themselves.

'Whether there's more to the statement "They shouldn't have touched her" than we were able to figure out.'

Another fifteen days went by. The police used whatever methods they could but nothing came out of Ashvamedha. They beat him, starved him, confined him to a smaller cell but nothing worked. He only laughed at the end of every day. It not only frustrated the police but also irked UKC. Never before had he waited for a criminal to confess in order to unravel the mystery, because so far he had successfully cracked every case.

It was close to ten at night. Neema brought his usual Scotch. She sat drinking rum next to him. UKC was brainstorming; maybe he had missed a clue. Then he smelt something burning. He glanced at Neema.

'I forgot about the milk!' She ran to the kitchen. Usually, she never made such silly mistakes. But UKC wasn't interested in the milk. He was interested in the word she had uttered: *forgot*. Unknowingly, she'd unlocked a certain 'what if' thought in UKC. The moment she came back, he asked her to call up Abhay. She dialed his number and brought the phone close to him.

'Hello,' Abhay said.

'Abhay, I'm really not sorry to call you at this hour.'

'What happened?' Very rarely did UKC call. Usually, it was Neema who called and passed on the necessary information.

'My instinct says I now know why Ashvamedha Chauhan hasn't confessed anything till now.'

Abhay was already interested.

'I was wondering about what Sama's brother said. That she had called them from the train but never came home? And in one of the videos, Ashvamedha said that she had gone missing from the train? I didn't think it was very important until now.'

'So, what have you arrived at?'

'Isn't it possible that Ashvamedha has forgotten about something that might have happened in the train that night? All he remembers now is that Sama went missing. Whatever little I know of psychology, it tells me that repressed memories often manifest themselves through aberrant behaviour.'

'Aberrant behaviour such as . . .'

'Like staying with the dead body of a loved one, pretending that they are alive.'

Abhay thought for a moment. It could be a possibility worth exploring because so far nothing had worked out.

'What if this has indeed what has happened? Then? How do we make him remember what he has forgotten?' Abhay asked.

'Meet me first thing tomorrow morning,' UKC said.

The next day UKC explained to Abhay what he had on his mind.

'We will need a psychotherapist to make Ashvamedha undergo regression therapy, which might allow us a peek into his repressed memories. The therapist would take him to that night in the train. If he has repressed anything from that night, it might surface. If nothing happens, we can at least be sure that he is telling the truth. That he indeed doesn't know beyond what he has confessed till now. Perhaps Sama indeed went missing and he later found her body.'

It took Abhay a day to fix an appointment for Ashvamedha. The therapist studied his case first, had a few preliminary sessions with him and then finally proposed that the main session be held in his clinic. Abhay and Vivek were present and so was UKC through a live video conference. Nothing was important enough for him to step out into broad daylight. The therapist drugged Ashvamedha first and then hypnotized him into closing his eyes. He told him to forget about his present surroundings, while whispering into his ears about the night Ashvamedha was in the train with Sama to Lucknow.

'What happened on that night in the train, Ashvamedha? Try to remember. Think. Just think, immerse yourself, let loose . . .'

Half a minute later, Ashvamedha frowned.

* * *

Ashvamedha's Talk During Regression Therapy

'We were happy. Sama and I. Life had turned out the way we had wanted it to. Sama and I were visiting her home town Kakori for Eid. I really respected the way her family had accepted me even though I belonged to another faith. The same was true for my parents. They never treated Sama differently.'

'Were you talking about this on that night as well?' the therapist asked as softly as possible.

'Yes. We were talking about it that night on the train. How lucky we were. She'd prepared kebabs for us for dinner in the train. She was a pro at it. We even discussed the possibility of opening a restaurant in Delhi selling Kakori kebabs exclusively. After dinner, we went to sleep. She was on the lower berth as she felt suffocated sleeping on the upper berth. So I'd gone up. We were traveling in an AC two-tier.'

'Then?'

'I woke up in the wee hours. The train had stopped at some railway station. I don't remember which one. I climbed down from my berth to go to the loo when I saw Sama lying on her berth, wrapped in a dirty piece of cloth. Only that cloth, nothing else was on her. There were bruises on her forehead and dried blood on her nose. I was stunned. I was sure it was a nightmare. But no, I was alive and this was real. My body started shivering. I quickly switched on the lights. I kept calling her name but she didn't wake up. A sticky substance was smeared all over the cloth. I understood it was semen. It was difficult for me to get a grip on myself. The train started to pull out of the station but I couldn't bear to see her like that. She was uncomfortable. I knew it. Something had to be done. But what? I lifted her up in my arms and somehow managed to get down from the train, forgetting about our luggage. I spotted a tap at a distance. I took her there and, turning the knob on, washed the semen off her. A few people gathered around me but nobody came forward to help. My mind had gone totally numb. My limbs were frozen. Someone said I should take her to the hospital. Someone said I had already destroyed the evidence.

Someone was asking who the woman was, where did I find her? I broke down. It was while I was howling that I finally accepted that Sama Akhtar, my wife, the love of my life, had been brutally gang-raped in a moving train at night while I was asleep. They must have muted her, taken her away and then dumped her on the berth. I don't know . . .'

'What happened then?'

'I was angry, but more than that I felt humiliated and defeated. I wanted to burn everything down but I had to take care of Sama. In my heart, I knew she was dead. But my mind didn't let me accept it. I took her to a nearby hospital. I didn't tell them anything fearing they would call the police and delay her treatment. They admitted her but told me that evening that she was brain-dead. My Sama . . . with whom I was in the process of building a world full of happiness . . . was brain-dead.

'I brought her to New Delhi and admitted her to a bigger hospital. I knew by then that my chances of a police complaint had gone forever as all the evidence had been erased. But at that point, I only wanted Sama to get better. To come back to life, to talk to me, to touch me and tell me she was all right, that our world was all right. Every night that I spent in the hospital, hoping desperately for her to recover, I kept questioning myself, what was happiness? Was it something that could be destroyed so easily? One train ride and now she wasn't with me any more. She'd been brutally snatched from me. And returned in a form that I didn't know what to do with. The thought disturbed me deeply. A month later the doctors at the hospital gave up.

You know the irony? I had to remove the oxygen support myself for the authorities to declare her dead. I removed the life support; I killed her! With my bare hands, I killed the woman who meant everything to me. I had been her life once. She had been mine. I felt so emasculated. So helpless. So insignificant. I brought Sama home, plastered her and promised her I wouldn't ever let her go. I don't know what the police say but she is alive. They don't believe me. But I know she is alive. We talk all the time about the past, the present and the future. How could she be dead?'

'Then what happened?' the therapist egged him on.

'I went back to work to resign and that's where I learnt who had raped her and why.'

'Who and why?'

'I was working on a project for an oil company. I was supposed to supervise the petrol pumps around Hisar in Haryana and seal the ones that illegally marketed petrol. I'd told my seniors to seal three of them; I had submitted detailed reports. I was ballsy enough to bust the petrol mafia operating in that area and expose how many of our own seniors were working hand in glove with them. I was even willing to be the whistle-blower. Sama was so proud of me. There were three other people in that project with me—Parth Basu, Adhik Sharma and Satyam Vishwanath. I had studied with them. Before they could support my claims, the mafia got to them first. Their mouths were shut with money and threats. They tried bribing me as well but it didn't work. Not only did those three bastards sell out, but they also told the mafia about my one weakness: Sama. It were members of that mafia gang who gang-raped Sama to teach me a lesson and force me to back out. I had never backed out of any situation in my life. I had taken a stand no matter the consequences. But I wasn't prepared for this. The mafia could teach me a lesson only because of those three bastards. And you know what? They shouldn't have touched her!'

'Anything else?'

Ashvamedha went quiet for some time. Then he spoke.

'I blew up those three petrol pumps. Nobody could link me to it. But I had to get to those three bastards. So I thought of a foolproof plan, but I needed a couple to execute it. I joined a school soon afterwards to sustain myself and Sama, and my plan. As luck would have it, one day at the birthday party of a student of mine, which was thrown at the food court of a mall, I overheard a young couple crying over the fact that they couldn't ever be together. I left a note saying if they wanted their love story to have a happy ending, they should call me. And they did call. I explained to them what they had to do. I would sponsor everything. And if they did what I wanted them to, then I would make sure they lived together, forever. They initially backed out, but later called me back after a fortnight. Perhaps they had no choice. I was their last hope. Their only conditions were that they wouldn't kill anyone and that the girl wouldn't sleep with anyone. The boy might if it were necessary. I agreed to their conditions. In return, I only had one. I needed six months of their lives exclusively for this. I used them to plant motives in Kashvi, Dhrithi and Sanisha's minds. I pitted the husbands and wives against each other. I attacked both Parth and Adhik, while

I made sure Dhrithi became my pawn for Satyam. I wanted them to be brain-dead as well. I wanted to make their families suffer. They had destroyed my perfect world. I damaged theirs with a perfect plan. They screwed up my world. I fucked up their universe.'

The session was over.

11

A week had gone by. Ashvamedha had been shifted to a government mental asylum for treatment. He would then be tried.

It was clear that while one part of Ashvamedha hadn't been able to come to term with Sama's gruesome death, the other had meticulously planned the revenge. He still believed that Sama was alive and that the police kept her away from him because he had tried to kill Parth, Satyam and Adhik.

Time passed. Abhay and Vivek moved on to other cases, knowing fully well that in this world justice wasn't always served the right way.

UKC wasn't able to forget Ashvamedha. One night as Neema was helping him sip his Scotch he said, 'I wish I hadn't suggested the regression therapy. For the first time, a criminal has made me feel guilty about my decision. I know it helped us in closing the case. What appeared to be the perfect crime has now been solved. But it made me think. What's justice? Certain acts can't be undone. The one who committed a crime can be punished, that's all. But is that enough? Why was Sama Akhtar subjected to such brutality? She didn't rub anyone the wrong way. All Ashvamedha was doing was his duty. He was being honest. We teach kids to be honest but have we built a system to award those who are? I think we are full of contradictions. Ashvamedha's decision to be an honest, upright citizen turned out to be a drop in the ocean. It created a ripple effect. And see what that effect has engendered. Disgraceful!' He took another sip.

'That's why I despise humans. Scotch is better. Make me another peg, please,' he said. Neema, dutifully, poured another drink for him.

EPILOGUE

Sanisha had been in Bhopal for three weeks now. So far, no one in her family had confronted her about the past couple of months. But the cold treatment she received perpetually made her wish for them to blast at her and let go of the matter once and for all. But she knew they would not. All she had to look forward to was getting married to a family friend's son, whose father ran a business of foodgrains. Although the family had claimed that the son was a widower, rumour had it that his wife was alive and had eloped with one of his employees. Sanisha had nothing to say. At twenty-nine, according to the society she lived in, she was too old for good proposals. Their families had decided there would be no roka; they would be married directly. After their marriage, her husband would get a stake in her family's newspaper.

The wedding was scheduled to take place in a week. Sanisha showed no interest whatsoever. Most of the time she was lost in what she'd heard about Ashvamedha and Sama. A part of her had turned into stone after a phone call with ACP Abhay. She had only wanted to inquire about Ashvamedha. He told her everything. She was disgusted to know the role Adhik had played in the incident. She simply couldn't shut out the memory of Ashvamedha lying thrashed in the lock-up. The night before her wedding, while she was lying on her bed, she suddenly realized something. She sat up on the bed, and on a hunch, started packing. Once done, she wrote a note on a piece of paper and kept it on the bed under the pillow. It read:

Sorry, Papa. Sorry, Mumma. I may have been a bad daughter but I can't willingly be a bad wife. I don't belong here or to the life that you are pushing me into. I'm going where I belong. And probably to whom I belong. Don't worry, I won't ever come back nor will I ask for any help. You have already done enough for me. I will call you from time to time. If you can, please do respond. My soul will be at peace.

Sanisha sneaked out of her house, called an Ola and left for the Bhopal Railway Station. There, she took a train to New Delhi.

Sanisha arrived at the mental asylum during visiting hours a day later. She was taken to Ashvamedha's cabin. As he didn't create any trouble, he hadn't been chained. He was sitting on the bed, his knees drawn up to his chest. He looked at her.

'How are you?' she asked. He didn't say anything.

'I realized something last night, Ashva. If I could dedicate the prime of my life to an asshole without blinking an eyelid, then I sure can spend the rest of my life for the man I've always respected,' she said, and thought, *and probably loved.* Ashvamedha still didn't respond.

264

'I will visit you every day here till you're all right. And when you are, I will take your case to Delhi High Court. I've talked to a lawyer from my NGO. She is willing to fight your case. Don't think I'm trying to redeem Adhik by doing this. My experience with him tells me that no man is worth any emotional investment. But I also want to prove myself wrong. I want to stand up for something, for someone. Like you did for Sama. I won't ever try to take her place. But I want to be with you. Beside you. That's all. I guess it will be the only medicine for the wound that Adhik has inflicted on me.'

Sanisha walked towards him. She could see his eyes were moist. She caressed his head and said softly, 'I'll be back tomorrow.' She left, not able to hold back her tears.

Ashvamedha turned his head to the right. Sama was sitting on the only iron chair in the room.

'What do you think of her?' she asked.

'I always knew she was different from the rest,' he said.

'True.'

'And I liked her even more when she said she wouldn't try to take your place.' Ashvamedha stood up and walked towards the chair.

'What's so special about me?'

Although a tear rolled down his cheek, he didn't feel it.

'You never make me feel alone.'

'One of those things you say.' He could see her blush.

'I mean what I say.'

'Okay, I have a request before you take a nap,' she said.

'What?' He looked at her with interest.

EPILOGUE

'Kiss me like you can't risk me.' He saw her close her eyes in anticipation.

Ashvamedha burst into a warm smile through the tears he weren't aware of. Deep in his heart, he knew they were the best couple ever.

ACKNOWLEDGEMENTS

A few of my college friends used to call me 'Howard Roark', after the protagonist of Ayn Rand's groundbreaking novel *The Fountainhead*, as I was always brutally honest to the extent of being self-destructive. What always bothered me was how the virtues taught in childhood were seldom followed in adulthood. Honesty was one such virtue. And so, I have always had a soft corner for individuals who suffer due to practising what had been taught to them in childhood without realizing that the real world has no place for such virtues. I've known someone who is like my fictional character Ashvamedha Chauhaan, and also observed at close quarters where honesty led him to. On the other hand, Sama Akhtar is a symbol for our conscience. Unfortunately, we have a social pyramid in place that we try to scale, but the first casualty during this climb is our conscience. And just like Ashvamedha, we all carry the corpse of our conscience and go through our lives pretending that it's alive. Ashvamedha, for me, is a symbol of courage. These two features—courage and conscience—I believe, is what makes us the ultimate creation.

This story has been the result of a phone call with my most favourite person—Milee Ashwarya—who wanted me to write a crazy crime fiction. The more we talked, the more I could see the characters shaping up in my mind. Thank you so much, Milee, for inspiring me and for everything else.

Indrani, my copy editor, I must tell you that the instinctive comments that you write while reading the manuscript are so entertaining, such as the one on Adhik, which totally cracked me up. Thanks!

To the entire digital team, marketing team and the sales team at Penguin Random House India—thank you so much for your faith every time.

My 'few' friends (who need not be named)—thanks for being there. Better stay there. Okay?

My parents—heartfelt thanks for never questioning me but always supporting me. I learn from you guys every day.

Paullomy—thanks for that phrase. I'm sure you know which one. I never knew it would feature in a book one day!

Ranisa—Quite ironical but your 'absence' has a magic. It creates a number of buds of life-queries in me, which later blossoms into answers whenever we converse. In UKC's words . . . if we can't see it, doesn't mean it's not there.

R—Thank you is a small word. But still for the lack of an alternative, thank you for allowing me a certain space within myself. It's not a space that creates distance between people. It's a kind of space that brings two souls as close as only souls can get. So, yeah, thank you so much, again.